We Have Heard

An Historical Fiction account of the story of Rahab

We Have Heard

Angela W. Buff

Word of His Mouth Publishers
Mooresboro, NC

ISBN: 978-1-941039-08-3
Printed in the United States of America
©2019 Angela Buff

Word of His Mouth Publishers
Mooresboro, NC 28114
www.wordofhismouth.com

Cover by Chip Nuhrah

The title of this book, "We Have Heard," was taken from a message on Rahab and the people of Jericho, which was entitled the same, by Evangelist Billy Abbott. As soon as I heard his message, I knew I had to use it to capture all the character that the story of Rahab has to offer. A special thank you to Brother Abbott for allowing me to use his title.

It seems a little strange that I dedicate my book on Rahab to my husband, John. Yet, it is entirely fitting as one of the quotes I use often in the story, "Our God never takes the easy way out," came directly from him. God saw past the imperfections of Rahab, allowed her to find forgiveness, and used her in the line of women He chose to send His Son to our world. My husband chose to look past my imperfections, choosing me to be his helpmeet and to help him build a life in this world. I am so thankful to the God we serve together, that He brought us together, and that He allows us to continue serving Him together. May you and the person you have chosen to spend your life with, or will choose, find peace and satisfaction in one another by seeking the perfect will of God in an imperfect world. And do not just "hear" the Word together but spread the Word together. "Our God never takes the easy way out," but He is the *only* way out! And tell the world together, all that

"We Have Heard."

Chapter One

Rahab tugged diligently at the covers surrounding her, attempting to reclaim at least a portion of them as her own. It wasn't an easy task under the thick arm of the burly man who had joined her the night before. Normally her guests, as she referred to them, enjoyed her pleasures then hurried to their own homes before morning. At times, however, either in a drunken stupor or perhaps overconfident in her attraction to them, they would pass out in her bed shortly after and remain there until morning. This had, on occasion, resulted in more discomfort than was necessary once she woke them. Once the sun had risen, they could no longer use the cover of darkness to cloak them as they made their way from her door into the streets of the city. She did not foresee this as a problem for last night's companion and, though she yearned for more sleep, she was somewhat uncomfortable with this man still in her bed. Then there was the bigger issue; he had taken all the covers for himself.

In an attempt to rise, she roughly shoved his arm from her shoulder and was about to speak his name when it occurred to her that she did not know it. She situated herself to better face the man, realizing as she did so, that she had no idea who she had just spent the night with. Looking at his sleeping face, mouth gaping and drool coming from the corners, she was sure she had seen him around town before, a traveling merchant perhaps, and was almost certain she had spoken to him on an earlier occasion when he had inquired as to the cost of her rooms. When he returned last night looking for board, she remembered playfully asking him if he planned to pass the night alone or if he would be requiring her company. His eagerness at her invitation was evident, and as with many of her other guests, exchanging pleasantries was not part of the deal. Typically, however, she at least knew the first name of the men she entertained.

Managing to rise, though awkwardly, she pulled a robe about her half-naked body and moved to the looking glass Nazim had brought to her on one of his recent visits. "Do not ever forget how beautiful you are," he had told her, "I know I never do."

Rahab looked at the vision of herself captured in the glass. She smoothed her thick black hair, which hung to her waist, still tousled and tangled from the night before. Her eyes were large and dark and held depth many men could barely resist, yet even she could see they lacked the life they had once held. She reached to touch her full lips, which were slightly tinted, mostly naturally, but remained somewhat swollen from the passionate, yet empty, kisses she constantly received.

"Who have I become?" she thought, sighing at her reflection in the glass. While many men considered her beauty unmatched, most women regarded her as horrific. A mythical siren many took great pains to avoid and from which they must protect their husbands and older sons. If it were not for the fabrics she dyed and the sewing she was capable of, her life outside the walls of her inn would cease to exist.

As a child, her mother had forced her to conceal her beauty, insisting on dressing her in robes far too big in order to hide her womanly curves once they began to develop. Her raven hair had been kept beneath a thick veil, and she was never allowed to go into the marketplace alone for fear that men would trick her into revealing her beauty.

Secretly, Rahab had longed for their affection as she became a woman but knew her father would beat her beyond recognition if she admitted it. They were poor, he had no money for a dowry, and he was far too proud to admit it. Though most men longed to be rid of their daughters, she knew her father had struggled to put food on the table each day, and he needed her assistance in what way she could offer−by

3

sewing and mending garments for the local villagers. Though her craftsmanship was superb, she typically earned no more than pennies here and there, yet her mother made sure every cent counted. Because of their impoverished situation, much of her young life was spent with downcast eyes, avoiding the face of strangers and clothing that she tripped and stumbled over as she walked.

All of that had changed when she met Nariman, so many years ago. Rahab closed her eyes at the memory, turned from her looking glass, and walked to the window of her chambers that overlooked the city streets. Nariman, with her gypsy-like qualities, beautiful clothing and hand-held instruments of music captivated her. Rahab remembered her and her mother passing this very inn on their way in and out of the village and many times Rahab had noticed the men lounging outside the door but never her father. Her mother would pay special attention to make sure his gaze never wandered in the mystical Nariman's direction.

On one occasion, Rahab slipped quickly away from her mother, allowing her curiosity to get the best of her. She made her way back through the corridors, sneaking in and out of alleys until she could peer through an opening in the stone wall. Tucked just out of sight of the villagers, Nariman was speaking with a man Rahab had never seen in town before, a man who was intently listening to whatever it was the woman was whispering to him. Her fingers toyed playfully with the latches on his vest as she tauntingly cast her eyes to his time and time again. Rahab watched as the man began leaning closer to Nariman, her body now pressed against the wall behind her. She allowed his advances, never moving to push him away, but continued to speak in hushed tones, which Rahab could not make out. Then, right before allowing his lips to touch hers, she pressed her hand firmly against his chest, stopping him from advancing closer.

Rahab could not hear what Nariman said to the man but saw the look of longing and frustration that crossed his face as he quickly slipped his hand into his pocket, pulled out two coins and handed them to her quickly. Dropping them into a satchel she had hung about her waist, she turned to escort him into the inner chambers of her inn but not before she turned in the direction where Rahab thought she was effectively hiding and looked her square in the eye. Rahab held her place but felt her breath catch in her throat.

Excusing herself from the man, Nariman walked over to the wall Rahab had been peeking through. "Come out, child," she had spoken in low tones. Rahab stepped around the corner into her presence, expecting a scolding and prepared to take it. She squared her shoulders and held her head higher than she had ever dared in front of anyone before. Nariman looked her up and down before reaching out and flicking the veil from her hair.

"Hmmm...as I expected," she began, "you are beautiful. Actually, you are mesmerizing and older than I first thought. Yes," she peered, "I've been looking for someone like you." Rahab noticed the slow and seductive way she spoke. "There is a lot of money to be made here," she whispered, leaning close assuring no word would go unheard, "in truth, more work than I can do alone. Yet, I believe you are extremely innocent." Nariman stepped back and looked at Rahab, her arms crossed as she studied the young girl in front of her. Her scrutiny made the young girl stand taller. "I have seen you about town bringing garments to the blacksmith and tentmaker have I not?"

"I make and repair torn garments," Rahab spoke firmly, yet she caught the tremor in her own voice. The man waiting for Nariman cleared his throat loudly, signaling his impatience.

"I am a little, um, busy, at the moment," she paused, turning to flash a smile in his direction, "but come back tomorrow and visit with me for a while. We have much to discuss." With that, Nariman turned and went into the doorway of the chambers where her visitor had been waiting.

Rahab had visited Nariman the next day and did not return until her satchel was full and she had plenty of money to supplement her father's income. She continued to abide with Nariman, at first only sewing sheer and fancy clothing in bright and vibrant colors for her new employer or mending those that had been tattered. It wasn't long after she had joined Nariman, however, that Rahab was introduced to some of the "newer guests" and had soon developed a reputation of her own, in some cases, even being requested in place of Nariman. Though they had never spoken of it, her parents speculated that her occupation had advanced beyond her dying and sewing fabrics, but never had they openly questioned her, for it kept plenty of food on the table.

Then, almost three years ago, Nariman had died. Rahab closed her eyes at the memory of her agonizing death, a single tear escaping her eye and sliding along her cheek. All activity at the inn had ceased during that time as Nariman cried out in both pain and the fear of dying. The town physician refused to treat her, for no one with a respectable reputation would be caught inside the inn, regardless of the circumstances. Rahab had been by her bedside when Nariman drew her last breath, tears streaming down her face as her only friend in the world lay begging her to make the pain go away. Finally, she had closed her eyes for the final time as her last painful breath wracked her frail body.

Rahab was jolted from the painful memory by a loud groan coming from the man still in her bed.

"What time is it?" he questioned, his voice thick with sleep and strong wine.

"Long past time for you to be gone," Rahab answered him with surety not bothering to turn and look at him from her place by the window. Her musings had left her in a bitter mood.

"That is not the words you spoke last night," he spoke slowly, and she could tell without looking back that he was still on the cot. "Join me again, and we shall make sure you earn your wages fairly," he continued.

"I have earned my wages fairly," she spoke firmly, "and it is time for you to leave." She glanced over her shoulder with an expression as stern as her voice.

"I believe I should be the judge of that," he answered, standing and stretching. His body repulsed her. Intuition and experience told her that getting him out of her house was not going to be a simple task.

"You will pay me what was promised," she shot back at him slowly and firmly as she turned to face him. "You will dress yourself, and then you will leave my home," she continued. "And you will do so now, without another word."

One thing Nariman had taught her was that she could never show fear. Once a man, any man, felt he had control of a situation, she was at his mercy. She had to display complete confidence in herself and in her abilities to protect herself at all times, whether during displays of passion, as she went about her life in everyday living, and in times such as this one when the job was done. Rahab had not left her place by the window, and though she held her composure, the fact that he was between her and the door out did not escape her.

The man laughed a loud, menacing laugh. "What are you going to do, harlot?" he scoffed, beginning to advance toward her slowly. "Run into the streets, plead your innocence, and cry out for help? Will the locals really believe it is your 'garments' I refused to pay for? Do you honestly believe they would take your charge of assault over my plea of innocence?" Rahab knew her back was against the wall, yet her stern eyes never left his face. The man who had approached her so cautiously and carefully the night before was extremely confident and sure of himself now that he had possessed her for a night.

A quick glance to her right allowed her to see the heavy clay pitcher she used to carry water into her room. As he closed the gap between them in sure, quick strides, he grabbed her arm with such a force she knew there would be a bruise. He pulled her body against his own so abruptly that her breath momentarily left her body. She reached as far as she could, trying to obtain the pitcher that lay just out of her reach. Burying his face in her neck, he tightened his arms about her waist and turned her body, attempting to force her back to the cot. Though his arms were tight about her waist, her arms were free. Ignoring her first impulse to struggle and fight against him, she remembered a trick she had learned from Nariman. Abruptly she stopped struggling and allowed her body to go limp, throwing the man off balance. That momentum was all she needed to be able to reach the pitcher. Grabbing it firmly, she smashed it squarely against the back of his head, the impact causing him to fall limp at her feet, both of them colliding to the floor in the process.

As she hit the floor, she heard pounding on the back door of her inn and the familiar voice of Nazim at the same moment. "Rahab, open this door at once, or I shall remove it!" he yelled through the closed portal. Her answer did not come quickly enough, and instantly, the door flew from its hinges where Nazim stood, filling the open portal, his sword drawn.

"I had the situation under control," she answered slowly, looking up at him from her place on the floor.

"I can see that," he answered sternly as the dust cleared, stepping over the unconscious man sprawled in front of her and helping her to her feet. "Rahab, how many times…" he began but stopped at her raised hand as she now stood directly in front of him.

"Not now, Nazim," she begged. The handsome man before her sighed, and she recognized the twitching in his jaw, a sign he was attempting to calm his temper and redirect his thoughts. Returning his sword to its sheath and crossing his arms, he pinched the corners of his eyes, took a deep breath, and directed his attention to the man he had just stepped over.

"Who is this?" he motioned to the heap on her floor which began to stir. Before she could answer, Nazim bent over and lifted the man's face from the floor by the hair of his head to see for himself. Not recognizing him, he slammed his head back into the floor with such force it knocked the stranger unconscious once again.

"He's a traveling merchant," she answered, not wanting Nazim to know that she had no idea of the man's name. "You know I do not reveal the identity of my guests," she smiled covering, "and you, Nazim, are bad for business," she added in an attempt to lighten his mood. She rubbed the hip she had landed on and inspected her arm for bruises. "Are you willing to help me get him out of here?" she asked.

Nazim pulled her to his side. "It depends," he chided her, "are you willing to allow me to rub that hip?" a smile played at his lips. "Perhaps I shall make up being bad for business by becoming your ONLY business."

Rahab pushed herself from his grasp, and he released her with ease. "Does the king know where you are?" she asked in a playful, mocking tone as she began to pick up shards of the broken pottery.

Realizing Rahab had ended the conversation he had not been allowed to start, Nazim moved to inspect the damage he had caused the door. "Never mind the king," he answered, "I am, after all, allowed to patrol the city wall when I am so minded."

"And the reason you were patrolling my inn?" she asked, picking up the last of the pottery.

Nazim shook his head. "Your 'inn' is inside the city wall, is it not?" he defended himself. "Besides, I was concerned about you," he continued nonchalantly as he turned from the door realizing nothing could be done to repair it. "I looked to your window as I passed and saw you gazing out. It is not a sight I typically see."

Rahab watched him as he came to stand before her. Though she was not short, Nazim stood at least a foot taller than she. "You make it a habit to look to my window?" she asked innocently.

"Rahab, you know I..." he searched diligently for the right words, "I care for your well-being," he stated simply, looking down at her. The stranger in her floor stirred again, moaning this time as he did so, and broke the sincerity of the moment. They turned in unison to stare at the sight.

"Does he have any clothes?" Nazim asked clearly frustrated at being interrupted again. Rahab moved to gather the few belongings he had thrown on a chair in the corner of her room. She picked up a small satchel and a tunic, which she threw in his direction.

"I will not tell you again," she informed the man who was now sitting up and holding his head in his hands. "Pay me the wages we agreed on and get out of my inn."

His eyes narrowed as he rose to move, this time determined to teach this wench a lesson for making such demands of him. What he had not counted on was the giant he now saw moving to stand behind her. Nazim was at least six-and-a-half feet tall, his arms twice the size of the beams that made up this inn. His hair was jet black and tied with a strand of leather at the back of his head, and a small, well-kept beard traced his massive jawline, meeting a thin beard perched neatly on his chin. Though he himself was not a small man, this man made him feel like a mere shepherd boy. He fell with a thud back onto the floor. Digging through his small satchel, he found two coins and threw them in her direction.

"There will be an additional charge," Nazim commanded, "for repairs to the door."

The man tossed an additional coin in Rahab's direction, refusing to make eye contact with Nazim.

"Do not think of ever coming near my inn again," she spoke sternly as she retrieved the coins from the floor. The man staggered to his feet and attempted to dress himself. Nazim stayed close to Rahab refusing to let this stranger even remotely close to her.

"Do not flatter yourself, whore" he jabbed, "I have no intentions of returning to such a pitiful establishment. The 'goods' here are well beyond used up."

Nazim took a simple step in his direction, causing the man to flee almost before his tunic was over his head. He tripped and stumbled over his feet but finally made his way down the hallway. From the sound of it, he tripped again on the stairs before he finally fell out into the street. Rahab turned to look out the window watching as he half-ran, half-limped through the ally way, never looking back at the villagers he almost ran over in his attempt to escape.

"He will do little trading here for a while," she spoke aloud. "It is evident now where he spent the night."

Nazim came up behind her and pulled her gently away from the window. *He does care for me*, she thought to herself as he pulled her body against his, and she laid her head against his broad chest. *Just not enough to show affection in front of the window where someone may see*, she realized. She sighed deeply, allowing herself to be cradled by her favorite person in the world. He made her feel protected and secure—attributes she did not want anyone to know she longed for, including Nazim.

"Rahab, how do you find these men?" he asked, lowering his chin to rest on the top of her head. Though she did not look up at him, she knew he was smiling.

"I do not have to look for them," she admitted truthfully, "they just seem to find me."

"I am glad that I found you when I did just a few minutes ago," he replied, and she felt the muscles in his arms tense. Rahab lifted her head and pulled back from his embrace enough so that she could look into his face.

"I had the situation under control," she argued.

"Because, evidently, a pitcher was nearby, and because I came in when I did," he argued back. "What would you have done had you not been able to defend yourself?"

Rahab thought for a minute before shrugging her shoulders. "I would have charged him extra," she spoke with surety.

Nazim released her so quickly that she almost stumbled. She watched as anger replaced his concern, saw the fire flood his eyes, and witnessed the muscles in his jaw clench.

"Rahab, you cannot be serious," he spoke, attempting not to raise his voice but containing it only barely. "I do not intend to seek you out only to find you have been killed by one of the fools you have entertained."

"And what do you intend to do about it, Nazim?" she asked pointedly. "Shall I pack my things and join you later before the king? Perhaps I shall become a seamstress for the queen? Will I be welcome in their courts? Will you, Nazim, once he and the queen realize their Chief Centurion keeps company with a harlot?" For reasons she could not explain, tears burned her eyes. She refused to let him see her weakness, refused to let him know that he had become a weakness for her. She turned her face from him to look out the window once again.

Nazim realized the corner he had been backed into. "I shall send a carpenter to repair the door," he spoke calmly, and though his voice was controlled, Rahab did not miss the anger still radiating through it. She did not turn but heard his footsteps as he made his way down the hallway and through the secret door, which led to an outer courtyard very few knew existed. He would exit from there, no one realizing from

where he had come, and answering her question
without speaking another word.

Chapter Two

Unlike Nariman had done, Rahab chose to occupy her time in ways other than just luring and entertaining men in her inn. Though no one asked her to mend their personal garments, her techniques for dying fabrics were unknown, and merchants would often trade with her in secret for her fine linens. Often, she would see her fabrics on the streets, the wearers never realizing it was she who had created them. She worked diligently and continued to supply her parents with enough money to feed themselves, her brothers, and her sister, who continued to live at home. Although the money she earned from her linens did not compare to that which she earned behind closed doors, it was enough to keep her parents from asking too many questions.

Rahab enjoyed watching the fabrics she dyed change from something so very plain and ordinary into something rich and vibrant with color. She continued to do her own sewing and had become quite skilled at needlework as well. She picked up a piece of linen, now a deep scarlet masterpiece and ran it through her fingers. This color was her favorite, and though it would bring much, she intended to save it for herself. A bit of needlework along the edges in a gold thread and the garment would be fit for the queen herself. And though Rahab knew she would never have an occasion in her life worthy of its wear, she could not bear to part with even the remnants of this particular fabric. Once again, she tucked the treasured piece away for some future use.

Thoughts of the future led to Nazim, and she quickly tried to drive them away. He was the highest-ranking soldier in the king's army; she a "secret seamstress" by day, but the village prostitute by night. Though she would secretly love to build a life with Nazim, she knew that would never be a possibility. His actions proved he cared for her, but they also proved he would never allow himself to admit that publicly. He had worked too hard to earn his place among the ranks in the palace. That was not something he was willing to throw away for anything—not even for her.

And so, their love affair would continue as it was. Nazim sneaking into her inn through the secret corridor when the mood so struck him and she filling many lonely nights without him—not alone but with wayward men and strangers passing through town willing to pay for what she could offer. Nazim often spoke of his desire for her to reserve herself exclusively for him but to do so would assure her dependence upon him, which was something Rahab was not willing to do.

Laying aside another piece of fabric, she gazed out the window of her room overlooking the village. Noticing the townspeople scurrying in and out of the city reminded her of an anthill she had kicked during her last walk to the flax field.

Their town was prosperous and well secured. Her inn, nestled inside the city wall, had windows facing both inside and outside the city. On one side she could see for miles past the flax fields, across the Jordan River, and to the mountain beyond. Inside the city, she could see the town's activity, all the way to the palace where Nazim spent the majority of his time when he wasn't patrolling the city, protecting the king.

Rahab allowed her mind to wander to life inside the Palace. Were she of a different profession, perhaps Nazim would invite her there.

"Why, yes, your majesty," she playfully bowed and spoke aloud imagining what it might be like before the queen, "this color would suit you beautifully." She held a piece of royal blue material in front of herself. "Me…no…I have no reason to wear such beautiful things. In your courts? You would have me become a member of your court? Oh, yes, your majesty, I would be honored." Again, Rahab bowed then laughed at her own antics. Dreaming never got her anywhere, and she gently tossed the fabric to a table nearby. A knock at her back door, which had been recently repaired, brought her from her musings.

"Rahab," the deep voice spoke. "Are you alone?" Rahab opened the door to find Nazim so close she was sure his ear had been touching the door. He propped himself in the frame of the portal, a serious look on his handsome face, and peered inside. "I heard voices."

"What you heard," she replied, stepping aside, allowing him passage into the room, "was a voice…not voices. My own. I often talk to myself for company," she smiled to him embarrassed by almost being caught at her musings and hoped he would not press the issue further.

"I knew it was unlike you to have guests this time of day," he spoke as he brushed past her, allowing one of his fingers to trace her jawline while his own face remained somewhat stern.

"It is also unlike you to come by this time of day," she responded, closing the door behind them. "You can see the door has been repaired nicely."

A few long strides allowed him to cross to the window facing the city, reaching from beside it to pull the shade. Not an indication he was paying her a visit for pleasure, just that he did not want to be seen inside her inn even if it was just to exchange pleasantries. It was a custom with Nazim she had come to accept.

"I did not feel at ease with the way we left things earlier in the week," he admitted. "You know I cannot publicly admit my affection for you, Rahab, yet I believe I have proven it to you over the years." As he spoke, he pulled a small box from inside his vest and held it out to her.

Rahab smiled in acknowledgment of the box but did not move to accept it. "You do not have to pamper me with gifts, Nazim. I understand your position. You have worked hard for your place in the palace. It is not worth losing due to the company you keep," she finished absolutely.

"Rahab, please," he continued. "I did not come here to fight but to make amends. You said I was 'bad for business,'" he quoted. "I only wish to make up for my," he paused as if looking for an accurate phrase, "over-protection of you."

Rahab looked to the box but still did not make a move to accept it. His declaration of being over-protective of her had not flattered her but, on the contrary, angered her. She had been secretly afraid of never seeing him again, and for that reason, perhaps it would be better if she never did. Yet, for reasons she wasn't quite sure of, she decided to push the issue a bit further.

"Over-protection," she stated, and her eyebrows reached her hairline. "You feel you are 'over-protective' of me. Need I remind you, Nazim, that you are 'protecting' me from men who are just like yourself? Do you remember how we met, Nazim?" she asked, approaching the giant in front of her. "You came to me for the

21

very same reason every other man who enters my door comes to me. To quench his physical desires." Nazim dropped his head to look into her face, and Rahab recognized the clenching in his jaw. Though she knew she was angering him, he was one man she was never afraid would physically harm her. It was the power he held over her emotions that she feared more. "Granted our relationship has evolved over the years into something more," she continued, "but it has yet to blossom into something beyond good paydays and expensive gifts," she finished. Nazim felt as if she had slapped his face, and his expression showed as much. Immediately she regretted her words, fearing she had gone too far, though she did not voice an apology.

Her heart thundered inside her chest, and she realized it was not fear of abuse that was erupting inside her, but more the fear of him leaving and never returning. Suddenly she could not imagine a life in which he was not a permanent fixture. She hated the mental attachment she had allowed herself to make to this man and immediately tried to think of a way to lessen the affects her harsh words had inflected. Quickly she decided on the one tactic that never failed. She allowed a tear to escape and roll along her cheek.

The tear brought exactly the reaction she was hoping for. Nazim pulled her to himself, embracing her fiercely and gently all at the same time. He simply held her for an instant as though he were afraid to let her go. She pulled back to speak again but did not have time as his lips reached down and claimed hers. Knowing she had won and would not lose him this day, she accepted his advances as he lifted her effortlessly and moved toward the cot.

Some moments later, Rahab lay, her head resting across his bare chest, his arm around her holding her close. Neither of them had spoken, but simply lay content in one another's company. "Rahab," he began breaking the silence from his place above her, "were circumstances any different, you know I would declare my love for you from the rooftops," he smiled, though he was completely serious.

"I believe the word love is a bit strong," she scoffed, "but none-the-less our circumstances are not different," she spoke, keeping her place on his chest. "You will always be a centurion of the king, and regardless of whatever comes, my past will always be as it is. I will never be able to escape the life I have lived or the life I continue to live, Nazim. And the palace will never be able to accept it." Rahab lifted her head now to look into his face. "It is not a decision I am asking for you to make, Nazim. There are no ultimatums here. I am not asking you to choose," she admitted to herself as much as to him. She would rather their relationship remain as it was than to lose him altogether. She rested her head again on his chest and snuggled back into his embrace. "Only to recognize our relationship for what it is." He kissed the top of her head.

"I wish things were different, Rahab," he spoke.

"No…you wish I were different, Nazim," her comment was not harsh, only factual. "You are perfectly comfortable with your life in the palace. If my life were not one of a harlot…" she allowed her sentence to trail off, shaking her head and moving to prop herself on her elbows. "Nevertheless," she continued, "I have flax to dry and you have a kingdom to protect. The king will be looking for his chief centurion before darkness falls, will he not?" Nazim pushed her hair from her face and kissed her bare shoulder.

"I suppose you are right," he smiled to her. Rahab pulled the covers close to her body and remained on the cot as he dressed himself, neither of them speaking until he turned to her, the box again in his hand. "I must go, but first," he bowed as he spoke, "for you, my lady." Sitting on the cot next to her, he held a small box out to her. His hair fell in ringlets around his face and shoulders, and Rahab could not help but chuckle at the adorable image he portrayed. She pulled the coverings tighter about her body as she sat up and accepted the box. She knew before she opened it that something beautiful lay inside.

As she cracked the lid, she could not help but gasp at the treasure it held—a simple, yet beautiful, ruby pendant surrounded by tiny diamonds and held on a thin chain of pure gold. It was not overly large, but the craftsmanship and quality were superb.

"Nazim, I do not know what to say. This is far too priceless a gift for me to accept. Where in the world did you come across such an exquisite piece of jewelry?"

He began to remove the necklace from the box. "In regard to your earlier comment, Rahab, love is not too strong of a word to describe my feelings for you. It is just something I cannot declare aloud," he spoke, pulling her hair to the side and fastening the necklace behind her neck. "I may not be able to take you to my home and make you my wife, and I may not be able to convince you to allow me to be your exclusive guest," he smirked, "but I do love you." With that, he kissed her forehead, picked up his belongings, blew a kiss in her direction, and walked out the door.

Rahab stared at the closed portal and fingered the pendant resting on her chest. The gift was overwhelming, but her realization even more so. "Just not enough," she spoke aloud tears rolling along her face. "It will never be enough."

Chapter Three

Rahab pulled firmly, urging the flax from its roots. It was no easy task, but the weather as of late had been on her side, and she was able to harvest much from her small field just outside the gates of the city. Here she could easily keep to herself; the other fields around her far enough away that she did not have to correspond with the owners. The drab clothes she wore to glean the flax helped hide her identity as well. She had heard comments in passing, those regarding her as "the mystery woman," but in all her time no one had ever approached her while she was in her field.

The days were growing shorter, and she must get her harvested reeds to the rooftop of her inn before darkness fell. It would be the fourth bundle she had carried up today, and her body ached in protest as she flung the heavy reeds across her back once again and made her way back to her home.

"Funny, Nazim is never around to help me in these situations," she thought aloud as she struggled with the bundle up the steps to the roof of her inn. With great relief, she allowed the bundle to fall with a thud before cutting the bindings and allowing the reeds to scatter across the rooftop. Glancing at the placement of the sun, she realized she needed to hurry to get herself cleaned up before tonight's guest, a regular, would arrive.

As she looked out across the Jordan River, she shielded her eyes to get a better view. Movement on the other side of the river had caught her eye, but she could not make out what it was. A caravan of travelers, perhaps? Shrugging her shoulders, she went downstairs and inside her room.

She had begun to heat the water earlier, and the temperature was perfect. She sank into the deep tub she used for bathing, allowing the warmth of the water to ease into her joints and muscles. As her body began to relax, the day's activity in the field began to seep away, and her lids grew heavy.

She was not sure how long she had been soaking there when she felt a gentle kiss on her forehead. Jolting awake with a start, she sloshed water all over the floor and all over Nazim who stood directly over her.

"Nazim! What are you doing here? What time is it?" she asked, jumping out of the water as she grabbed a thick towel and quickly wrapped it around herself. "How did you get in?"

Nazim stared at the image in front of him as Rahab quickly braided her wet hair until it hung in a thick rope across her shoulder. She was beautiful.

"I knocked, but you did not answer. I was worried, so I let myself in," he stated matter of factually as he took a large bite from a piece of fruit he had confiscated. Rahab quickly crossed to her looking glass and began to powder her face.

"Let yourself in?" she half questioned as she glanced outside to see the placement of the sun. Her guest would be here very soon, and she knew she really had no time for small talk. She would find out how Nazim "let himself in" later and dismissed her question for now.

"I came to make sure you had gotten in all of your flax today," Nazim continued, but Rahab could tell by his tone that there was more to his visit. He toyed with a tassel hanging from a cloth on the table.

"And..." she inquired simply as she applied tint to her lips.

"And," he continued, "to see if you heard any talk of interest in the fields today as you were about your business."

"Talk?" she asked, motioning for him to turn his back to her, which he did begrudgingly, as she dropped her towel and began to dress herself. He knew she never talked to anyone.

"What kind of talk?" she asked as she continued to dress.

"Rumors mostly," Nazim confirmed, turning to face her again as she tightened the belt of her robe. "But there is enough truth in them that I must insist you be extremely cautious over the next weeks. I do not feel at all comfortable with all we have heard." Rahab recognized something in Nazim's stature that she was unfamiliar and uncomfortable with. Caution, reserve, perhaps even fear?

She paused in front of him, holding a bottle of scented water, "Nazim, what exactly are you implying?"

"We have heard...rumors," he continued, "stories really, in the palace, of a company of people who have been wandering the desert for some time. 'God's people,' they call themselves. They are wandering slaves out of Egypt and have been led by a man called Moses, searching for their 'Promised Land.' In their search, they have overcome many men, declaring the lands they have overtaken as part of this land they seek. Supposedly, the God they serve has promised it to them. The man, Moses, has died, but a new leader, Joshua, has risen to lead them. Yet, we have heard, before Moses' death when he still led them, that their God allowed them safe passage across the Red Sea." Nazim toyed with the pendant hanging around her neck. She could tell he was trying to keep his conversation light, though there was something underlying in his tone. He was trying not to scare her, though she detected he was nervous about it himself.

"All right, they crossed the Red Sea. That is no small task I am sure, but as you said they are rumors," she both stated and asked, "and that this Moses is now dead?" Though she was curious as to his concern, she really needed to be getting on about her current business. Her guest would be here at any moment, and though she did not care for him personally, he was a regular, and he paid well.

"It is true, he is," Nazim continued, "But this Joshua was trained by Moses, and I do not feel he is one to be taken lightly. The king is a bit unnerved at all the talk, but I have assured him we are safe. Our walls are strong and virtually impassable." She recognized his uneasiness with the subject. He spoke clearly but stared past her as he did so. His mind was definitely on the tales he had been told.

"So, you feel we are secure, yet you are here asking me if I have heard talk? Nazim, what is it? What are you keeping from me?" Rahab asked pointedly as she continued to stand directly in front of him.

He was momentarily distracted at the beauty in front of him and suddenly realized it. He did not know why he had even bothered to tell her of the company of slaves. He reached out to pull her to himself, but she dodged his grasp.

"Why are you getting so made up? Who is coming?" he began as a knock at the door interrupted their conversation.

"You should go," she spoke quietly though matter-of-factly.

Nazim rolled his eyes as realization dawned.

"Can he not go instead?" he asked impatiently. "Let me be your guest tonight," he pleaded as he attempted to draw her to himself again.

"Unless you want to be caught in my inn, you should hide back here until I can distract your officer," she spoke quietly as she ushered him into a small back room where she kept her dyes and fabrics.

"My officer!" Nazim asked pointedly as her words registered. "One of MY men," he asked in anger. "Who is it?"

"Get in there," Rahab pushed him and grinned sheepishly pulling the door closed as Nazim continued to speak.

"I shall have his head!" he called to her from the closed door in an exaggerated whisper.

"You look stunning this evening," Nazim heard the mystery guest proclaim as Rahab opened the outer door, and though the voice was muffled coming through the closed portal, Nazim could tell exactly which of his men it was. The one soldier he hated almost as much as he hated the man who had attacked Rahab earlier.

"Make yourself comfortable by the cot, and I shall join you in a moment. I need to freshen up just a bit more," she lied as she turned away from him.

"You look and smell amazing already, and I am in a bit of a rush," he continued as she escaped his presence, "do not take long," he commanded. She quickly rounded the corner and crossed to the door where Nazim was hidden.

"Go," she whispered, opening the door and motioning him out.

"Seriously? Jakabed? The man is a joke! A coward! I could take him out right now, and no one would ever be the wiser." Nazim whispered, stepping from his hiding place with his hand on his sword.

"Rahab...I am waiting..." the voice called from the other room, and Nazim flinched as he heard the man's sandals hit the floor with a thud. Nazim began to pull his sword from the sheath, "Let me at him!" he whispered harshly, taking a step in that direction.

Rahab stopped Nazim with both hands to his chest. "Out, Nazim. Now!" Rahab commanded him, whispering equally as harsh and pointing toward the door.

"I shall double what he is paying you," Nazim whispered to her, and there was not only anger but also a longing in his voice she could not miss. "I shall triple it," he finished. He honestly wanted her to take him up on his offer. Searching his face in surprise, she almost gave in, not for the money, but simply at his request. Quickly, she decided against it, realizing the picture that would portray, the picture that she could depend on him and him alone.

"Nazim," she barely spoke but was completely serious, "Go."

He watched her intently a moment more, then turned and slipped out the door. Rahab stared at the barely closed portal before her guest approached her from behind.

"There you are," he laughed, grabbing her around the waist. "I thought you were playing games with me."

"Now, why would I do such a thing to such a loyal customer?" she chided him sweetly. "Forgive me for keeping you waiting, Jakabed. Come, let us get down to business."

Less than an hour later, Jakabed was preparing to leave but was taking his time since it was hours before the sun would break over the horizon. Rahab could not get her mind off the conversation she and Nazim had begun before Jakabed's appearance and recognized this man was not in nearly as big of a hurry to leave as he had been for her to earn her wages.

"So," she began sweetly as he was lacing his sandals, "I suppose things at the palace are pretty boring these days. You have not missed an appointment in quite some time." Rahab had released her braid and now pulled her brush through her hair, attempting to look as if she was just making general conversation. She saw the look that crossed Jakabed's features. "That look was interesting," she chided, laying down her brush and turning from her looking glass to face him. She knew exactly how to get the information she sought from this man.

Crossing behind him, she began to massage his shoulders. "Still tense?" she asked from his back. The man straightened and smiled over his shoulder at her.

"No, no, do not question your abilities to ease tension, Rahab," he laughed patting the hand on his shoulder, "but I would not say life at the palace is boring."

"Oh?" she asked simply, continuing to massage his shoulders.

"It is just rumors we have heard circulating lately of a company of people coming through the desert in an attempt to reach, what they call their "Promised Land."

"Their Promised Land?" she questioned pretending it was the first time she had heard the statement. "And these rumors pose a threat for our city?" she asked innocently.

"Yes," he continued, "apparently the land they seek rests in Canaan."

"Our walls are strong and our soldiers stronger," she smiled continuing. "No company of people will have the ability to overcome them." Rahab was confident in her statement, though for the second time today, something about this felt different. She spoke the words in surety, but inside, she wondered what about this made her nervous.

"This group could be worth watching out for," he answered thoughtfully tilting his head. "This company has crossed over the Red Sea."

"So, they have crossed the Red Sea," Rahab scoffed from her place at his back still not sure why this was such a great feat.

"On dry land," he finished. He felt her fingers pause in their massage and knew he had caught her attention. He continued, pleased with himself for surprising her. He did love sharing information when he felt safe doing so, and he knew Rahab was a soul of discretion. "Apparently, they were escaping from the Egyptians, and as the story goes, their leader raised his staff, the sea parted, and they crossed over on dry land. Once they were safely across, the sea fell back in upon their enemies, destroying them all." Rahab stopped massaging.

"How is that possible?" she scoffed again.

"They give credit to their God, Jehovah. And then there is the fact that they have completely overtaken both Kings Sihon and Og along with the others who were in their path" he continued.

"Sihon, of the Amorites?" Rahab left his shoulders and came to stand directly in front of him. She knew those were not small areas to overtake. Until now she had assumed it was only trivial lands they had claimed.

"Yes, as well as Og of Bashan." Jakabed seemed to be lost in his thoughts for a moment before turning and producing the coins he owed. "For your time," he spoke, breaking his trance with surety as he handed her the coins. Rahab took them without a word her mind on bigger issues than money.

Sihon and Og. No wonder Nazim had seemed troubled. Jakabed let himself out as she stood staring out the window.

Chapter Four

Salmon rode into camp quickly but not with such a pace that would bring alarm to his leader and friend, Joshua. He had been venturing forward, scouting terrain and looking for evidence of any soldiers who could have been warned of their coming. He was pleased he had seen nothing.

Before his stallion came to a stop, he slid from the back of the magnificent beast he had raised from a colt. He had been born in the wilderness and needed special attention to survive. Attention Salmon had given him despite the chiding and ridicule of his fellow Israelites.

"We do well to eat from the manna the Lord sends us ourselves, yet you concern yourself over a horse?" they would shout. "Let that beast die and worry not over him," they would continue. More than once, Salmon had stood by the animal's side to keep protestors away, and his efforts had paid off. Indeed his horse was now the strongest in the camp which had served them all well on more than one occasion of battle.

Salmon found Joshua by a campfire alone and in peace. No doubt he was praying, as he often did, searching for God's direction on their next moves in the coming days. He hated to interrupt, but he knew Joshua had been waiting on word from him.

"I find nothing that would speak of an immediate threat, Joshua," he spoke as he approached.

"Salmon, my friend," Joshua stood to greet him as he approached. "You have returned. Our camp is safe, then, so rest yourself," he motioned as he took his seat again by the fire. "Caleb will be here soon, and we can discuss our plan."

Salmon situated himself by the fire, taking a piece of manna as he did so. Many grumbled over their meager fare, but he had come to love it. The taste of honey reminded him of God's love and attention to detail. The meal He had continued to provide for them daily could have been stale and dry and would have provided just as much nourishment as they needed; yet, He chose to include a bit of sweetness for nothing more than their pleasure.

Salmon noticed Joshua was unusually quiet and wondered over his leader's musings. Joshua was wise beyond his years, thanks to his earlier training from Moses. Salmon knew that Moses was missed, and he himself had always admired the man beyond words, but no man finer than Joshua could have been chosen to continue to lead their people after Moses' death. Though others grew discouraged and scoffed, Salmon had no doubt they would indeed enter the Promised Land under the direction of Joshua and the protection of Jehovah God.

Salmon stood as he heard Caleb, Joshua's dearest and most trusted friend, approach. The men exchanged the usual pleasantries and then situated themselves again. Joshua was the first to speak.

"Salmon assures me there is no immediate danger to our camp, yet I cannot rest easy until we know more. The soldiers of Jericho are strong and ruthless. They have been trained well. I do not doubt that we can overtake them; God has shown what He can do using us as His meager vessels already. But I just feel the need to know more before we advance forward."

"We have never questioned you, Joshua," Caleb encouraged him.

"Tell us what you need, and we shall do our best to obtain it," Salmon continued.

"I would like to send two men into the city. Travelers and merchants come and go through the city gates daily, so I do not foresee that as a task hard to accomplish. Our God works in miraculous ways, yet we have heard of the walls that reach to the sky, and obviously, we can see them from here," Joshua continued motioning into the darkness. "What I want to know is what sort of structure lay inside those outer walls. I want to know what the people within those walls are hearing. Are they preparing for us? Have they heard of the miracles we have witnessed? I want to know what lies before us, so that I may know how to pray for their deliverance unto us."

"I will go," Salmon spoke up immediately. Joshua reached to clasp his shoulder.

"I had no doubt you would be the first to offer," he thanked his faithful warrior. "But I do not want you to go alone. Choose another man to accompany you. I do not know what you will face, and if you will be welcomed as a merchant or observed as a threat."

Salmon thought through those in their camp closest to him. Immediately, Garrick came to mind, and he voiced his thoughts.

"He is quick with a spear when needed, yet stealthy and dependable," Salmon explained. "Allow me to go alone when day breaks. I would like to get across the river and closer to the city on my own accord to watch the people who come and go. I shall return before nightfall, then, under cover of darkness the next night, Garrick could accompany me, and we shall approach the gates of the city. We shall enter as the others do, find the answers to the questions you speak, return to you, and tell you all we have found." Caleb nodded in approval as Joshua stood.

"Very well. Proceed with caution, Salmon. I feel we are very close to another miracle and to finally reaching the Promised Land for which we have searched for so long. The people grow restless and discouraged. I fear how much more they can take."

Salmon agreed as he stared into the fire. He too felt a miracle was about to take place, yet there was another notion, something more he felt was about to transpire. He just had no idea what it could be.

Rahab gathered the coins she would take to her father's house and closely pulled the drab veil she used to conceal her identity around her face. She hated the muted browns and tans she wore today, much more preferring the vibrant colors she wore on a daily basis. However, those colors would expose her identity, and she would not be treated kindly as she moved about the city. Yet today the weather was unusually warm and these fabrics so much thicker than the disguise she wore when gathering flax. Now, only her eyes were exposed. She would move quickly to the other side of the city, deliver the coins to her family, and return to the safety and solitude of her inn. She would exit through the inner courtyard Nazim used for his visits so no one would witness her coming and going.

She moved into the city street with her "basket of goods" hanging from her arm and proceeded down the dusty roads. The thick crowds in the streets caused the heat to smother her. She much preferred viewing the streets from her window above than being herded through them like cattle. People bustled about, busy in their daily chores and, as planned, no one paid her any extra attention as she made her way through the crowd. She paused only for a second when she saw Nazim on patrol. It always took her off guard to see him outside her inn, but she was pleased when she realized that even he did not recognize her today. He barely noticed "the woman" who passed by him as he strode through the streets maintaining peace and order.

Out of habit, she reached up to feel the pendent beneath her robes. It reminded her of her relationship with Nazim, strange as it may be, and somehow, she felt closer to him by wearing it. Perhaps that is why she had not taken it off since the day he had placed it about her neck. She felt a comfort knowing it was there even now when even he wasn't aware how close in proximity the two of them were.

Rahab hurriedly made her way through the town and down crowded alleyways until she reached the location of her parent's home. The walk was a bit of a long one through the city, yet she was strong and made the journey quickly. Here she could remove enough of this clothing so that she could breathe freely.

She knocked on the door out of respect and waited until she heard her mother's greeting to enter. Opening the heavy wooden door, she was met with hugs and excitement from her younger sister and two younger brothers. Quickly, she placed her basket on the table and removed her veil, instantly feeling the cool air refresh her face. "Finally," she exclaimed as her mother handed her a cloth to wipe the sweat from her cheeks and chin. "It seems so warm today," she admitted as she continued to unwrap the extra cloth from her head where it concealed the mounds of hair piled on her head.

"Summer will be here before you know it," her mother stated, as she sat warm bread on the table. She had been expecting her oldest daughter at some point today, and her timing was impeccable.

"Did you bring us anything, Rahab?" her sister asked impatiently.

"Let me see what I can find in my basket, Amelia," she said playfully to the girl before her. Reaching in, she pretended to shuffle through numerous contents before producing a beautiful ribbon she had dyed just for her. It was the same shade of scarlet as the fabric she had decided she could not part with. It would look lovely in her sister's hair, which was as jet black as her own.

Amelia grabbed the fabric with a shriek of excitement. "Thank you, thank you, thank you, Rahab!" she exclaimed. "It's beautiful!!"

"You should wear that when you go to the well to draw water this afternoon, Amelia. That

45

should grab the attention of that handsome shepherd boy you have been rattling on and on about," their mother laughed.

"Mother!" Amelia protested, rolling her eyes.

"Do tell," Rahab chided. "I should like to hear all about this mystery shepherd?"

"Mother is trying to marry me off already, Rahab," Amelia pouted.

"Thanks to your older sister and her hard work with her fabrics, we may be able to afford a dowry enough to marry you off," her mother laughed. Rahab shook her head, knowing her mother would never admit to how she had really made her living over the years. However, Amelia becoming of age had been enough to get her mother and father off the subject of she herself finding a husband. They held hope since her "vocation of choice" had never been admitted to, yet Rahab knew she would never marry. No man in his right mind would want a woman such as she had become. She shook her head to clear her musings and to focus on the family who loved her. She had no time to be dwelling on things she could never change, and the time she had with them was always too brief.

She continued through her basket and handed each of her brothers a piece of fruit for themselves, the bag of coins going directly to her mother. Her mother took the bag and hugged her tightly. "Thank you, daughter," she said from the embrace they shared.

"Where is Father?" Rahab questioned, breaking their hold.

"Did I hear someone asking of me," he asked while coming through the door at just that moment. "Has at last my prodigal daughter returned?" he laughed pretending to be shocked. Rahab embraced the first man she had ever loved.

"I have missed you, Father," she admitted sincerely.

"Your mother told me you would be along soon," he joked, "but I told her you had flown from our grasp never to return."

"Father, I was here just two weeks ago," she laughed.

"True you were, but that seems a lifetime ago," he commented matter-of-factly.

Rahab took a piece of warm bread from the plate her mother pushed in her direction. "I made that just for you," she smiled, knowing it was her daughter's favorite. They visited for the next hour, catching up on family news before her father voiced a question that really caught her attention.

"Rahab, have you heard talk in the city of a coming war?" he asked sincerely. Her heart faltered once again, and she feared where this conversation was headed.

"A coming war?" she asked, "here in Jericho?"

"We have heard rumors," he began, "of a company coming across the desert overtaking any kingdom they come across. Apparently, their

God has promised them this land, and theirs is not a God to be trifled with."

Rahab did not wish to alarm her family, but she also did not want them to know about the rumors she had heard from Nazim and Jakabed. "But I don't understand," Rahab admitted, "what has that to do with us, with Jericho? We have been established here for hundreds of years."

Her father shook his head, "Apparently Jericho is part of this Promised Land they insist belongs to them," he finished. Rahab's father was not one to typically worry himself with petty tales, and the look of concern over the things he was actually sharing with his oldest daughter was evident on his face. She could tell that he had given much thought to the stories and was indeed concerned over what he had been told.

Had he known it was the third time she had heard these same rumors in just a few short days, he would have been even more alarmed. "Oh well," he continued with a wave of his hand, "let us not dwell on politics and war stories." His intention was not to alarm his daughter, but the look on her face indicated he had done just that. "Our city walls are strong, and we are well protected by the king and his centurions," he finished closing the matter.

"Especially Nazim," Amelia swooned. "Have you met him in the city, Rahab?" she questioned. "Is he not the most handsome man who has ever lived?" she sang. Rahab looked at her sister in surprise and then to the floor as she felt her face flush at the mention of his name, her fingers reaching for the neck of her tunic where her treasured pendant lay securely beneath.

"I, I know who you are speaking of," she stammered.

"I shall meet him one day," Amelia dreamed out loud as she danced about the room waiving the new ribbon Rahab had just given her.

"Not if your shepherd boy has anything to do with it," her mother laughed. "Out the door, all of you," she commanded. "Amelia, draw the water, boys do the barn chores. Out you go," she finished waving them out.

"I must go as well," Rahab's father stated as he arose. "I'll um…help the boys" he exclaimed kissing Rahab on the head and then her mother on the cheek. "I sense when there is 'woman talk' to be had," he laughed as he exited.

As soon as the door was closed, her mother turned to look at her. "I saw that look, daughter," her mother started pointedly, "and the flush of your cheeks."

"Mother, I am a grown woman with an independent profession of my own. I do not need a man to make my way." Rahab was doing her best to sound confident, but she could not stop the way her cheeks had flushed yet again.

"That may be," her mother continued, "but you do not blush like that when your sister mentions any other man in her musings. I dare say you know Nazim rather well or at least wish you did," she smiled.

"Mother, this is a topic I do not wish to discuss," Rahab admitted respectfully, though clearly serious. "I will confirm, out of respect to you, that I know Nazim. But I can also say, in complete truthfulness, that there will never be a union there. We are two completely different people in two completely different worlds."

"But, Rahab, though your father and I could not provide a dowry for you before, perhaps he and your father could work out something now…" Rahab took her mother by the shoulders and looked deep into her eyes.

"Mother, my way has been made. I have done well and provided not only for myself but for you and father and my siblings as well. I do not need a man," she stated simply, "nor do I want one." Rahab knew she was lying to her mother, but she did not wish for this conversation to continue any farther. Her relationship with Nazim was complicated and to divulge further information would mean telling her mother not only how well she knew him, but an admission to her "complete" profession as well - something she was not willing to do and honestly her mother was not willing to hear. "I have enjoyed our visit mother, but in a few hours it will be nightfall, and I must get back."

Rahab kissed her mother, accepted the bread she stuffed into her basket, wrapped herself again in her drab veil and coverings, and left with the promise to return again soon.

Chapter Five

Rahab knew she had a few hours before darkness when she began her walk toward home. Though she knew Nazim would not be happy with her and that she should stay within the city gates, she could not bear the thought of the crowded city streets again. Her conversation with her parents, especially her mother, had unnerved her, and she needed to clear her mind and refocus her thoughts. She wasn't sure on what that would be exactly but anything other than her relationship with Nazim being anything more than what it was.

With a plan in her mind to do just that, she turned down an alleyway that would lead her away from the center city streets and just beyond the city wall. She would hurry and not spend too much time outside the gates, but she longed to see the palm trees sway in the gentle breeze and craved the solitude they promised. She knew that only a few moments in that setting would make her feel herself again.

Stepping beyond the wall made her feel free. Free from the life she lived, free from Nazim, free from herself. A whole new world lay out there, and this time of day it was sure to be quiet. She strolled, still heading in the direction of her home while enjoying the peace the valley offered. Palm trees swayed in the late afternoon breeze, and the wind gently rustled the fronds creating the most soothing sound she had ever heard. She loved that sound.

Rahab leaned against the trunk of an obliging tree, pulling her veil free from her face while keeping her head covered. She closed her eyes, breathing in the fresh air and focusing on the sounds around her. Was there ever a sound so serene as the palm trees tossing gently in the breeze? The soothing rustle as the wind passed through the branches tossing them back and forth in a gentle motion. She focused intently on the peaceful breeze, allowing her mind to clear until another sound came to her ears. Someone was coming from behind her. Pulling her veil quickly over her face, she turned to the other side of the tree and stood at full attention, realizing too late that she had allowed herself too much time outside the city gates.

"Well, well, what have we here?" the man asked as he approached her with a sickening smile on his face. It took only a second for her to recognize the man as the same who Nazim had run from her inn just a few weeks before. He was not a merchant as she had expected - he was nothing more than a wanderer and probably a thief. He had not yet recognized her, and she intended to keep it that way.

"What is a lovely maiden like you doing outside the city gates all alone?" he asked menacingly.

"My brother," she began to lie, "asked me to wait here for him. He will return at any moment." She tried to sound confident though her voice faltered.

"Your brother," he laughed. "Come now. Surely you can do better than that. I think I have caught you daydreaming and alone outside the protection of the city. What do you have in that basket of yours?" he asked as he came close enough to snatch it from her grasp. She let the basket go, hoping that would satisfy him.

"Bread!" he scoffed, "no goods in here worth wasting my time on. But you," he spoke menacingly, "you look like something I might enjoy for a little while; let me see that face of yours," he smirked, as he tossed her basket aside and jerked the veil from her face. Rahab stood tall and attempted to slow her heart, which was now about to beat out of her chest. He burst into laughter when he realized who she was.

"Well, well, we meet again, harlot," he laughed as he began to circle around her as if she was his prey, "and if I am not mistaken, you owe me a bit of fun. Where is your 'brother' now?" he smirked.

"I owe you nothing," she spoke calmly and plainly though her heart continued to race. "You will not touch me again."

"Oh, I beg to differ," he argued, the sick smile leaving his face as it turned dark and menacing. He reached out before she could dodge him and grabbed her arm, pulling her to himself.

"Unhand me!" she yelled, unwilling to become a victim to the very man she had already been saved from once. As his arms encircled her waist, she went limp in an attempt to throw him off balance as she had done before. This time he was ready for her retaliation and moved with her, picking her up from the ground and throwing her against the tree. Her head struck the trunk, and in an instant, she felt blood begin to wet the back of her neck. She was not sure what happened next, only that the turn of events happened so quickly that she would replay them in her mind for years to come.

The man began to quickly advance to where he had flung her to the ground, but as he did so, he suddenly paused, falling face-first into the dirt. She watched him fall and gasped when behind him stood another man, a man she had never seen before. He was every bit as big as Nazim but with lighter hair and eyes.

"I believe you had asked him to unhand you, had you not," he clarified, rather calmly.

"I, I did," she stuttered trying to calm the whirling in her head as she slid up the bark of the tree attempting to stand on her feet, somewhat fearful of this unknown stranger before her.

"Easy," he advised stepping over the man in the dirt and reaching out to steady her. "You are bleeding," he observed gently, turning her face so he could see the back of her head. He quickly ripped a scrap of fabric from the bottom of his tunic to hold up to her wound.

"It, it is, I, I am fine," she struggled to get the words out taking the cloth from his hand and pressing it to the back of her head herself. The pain was severe.

"You have quite a bump there, but I do believe it is only a small cut. Still, I think you should rest here for a bit," he instructed, encouraging her to sit and rest against the tree.

"How do I know you do not intend to finish what my captor intended to begin?" she asked her jumbled head beginning to clear and coming to her senses. She asked the question but surprised herself that her fear over this handsome stranger had all but vanished.

"As Jehovah God is my witness," he spoke with surety, "I will do you no harm," he promised.

Sudden alarm flooded through her body. Jehovah God? He was one of the Israelites. One of the men Nazim, Jakabed, and her father had heard and spoken to her of. She thought of fleeing but was not sure her head was clear enough to allow her to move just yet. Perhaps she could gain information from him that would be helpful to her people. Slowly she sat back down and leaned against the tree. He knelt beside her.

"Did you kill him?" she asked outright looking past him to the man in the dirt.

Her rescuer laughed as he looked back over his shoulder. "Maybe, but I think not." He paused, a quizzical look crossing his features. "Although, I suppose I should check to see if I need to be digging a grave eventually. Yet, there is no reason he should live with what he had in mind to do." Rahab dropped her head. "I apologize," he spoke quickly. "I did not mean to embarrass you."

Rahab looked at him in surprise. If he had the slightest idea as to her profession, he would be the one embarrassed.

"I owe you a debt of gratitude," she admitted finally. "I have nothing to offer you except maybe some bread," she offered as she pointed to her basket still laying a few feet from them. He smiled genuinely at the beautiful woman in front of him.

"Bread sounds wonderful," he grinned, moving to get her basket. Picking it up, he started back toward her but stooped again. It was at that exact moment Rahab realized her necklace from Nazim was gone. She gasped at her tunic and searched the ground around her frantically without rising.

"Is this what you are searching for?" he asked, holding the necklace out to her. "It was lying just there." He spoke so kindly that she smiled at him. Her smile all but stopped the beating of his heart.

"Yes, thank you," she breathed a sigh of relief as she quickly took the necklace from him. "It must have gotten pulled off during the struggle."

"That must be from someone pretty special," he began, though she could tell the statement was more of a question. "A gift from your betrothed perhaps?"

Rahab smoothed the pendant she now held in her hand and looked up at him. "No. I am not betrothed, but it was a gift from a, a," she struggled to find the right words, "a dear friend," she finished.

The stranger smiled, and she noticed how his grin took in his entire face. Even his eyes seemed to smile.

"So, would your 'not betrothed, but dear friend' mind if you broke bread with me, your rescuer?" he laughed, handing her a piece of bread.

"No, I suppose not," she stated as she took the bread he offered but was quite sure she may be lying. "I do thank you, for saving me from…" she let the sentence trail off as she pointed to the man who had yet to move from his place on the ground. The handsome stranger shrugged his shoulders, dismissing the gesture as though it were just a typical occurrence.

"Do you know him?" he asked.

"I do not know his name," she answered truthfully, "though I have seen him before.

Speaking of names, I did not have the privilege of obtaining yours," she spoke quickly, hoping to change the subject.

"Salmon," he answered. "And you are?" he questioned in return. Rahab thought for a minute before answering. Should he know her name? It still would not give him her true identity for he knew nothing of their city. And what harm would come from him knowing her name?

"I am Rahab," she answered truthfully before she could convince herself otherwise.

"Well, Rahab," he continued, "what brought you out here all alone?" he asked, taking a bite of bread. "This is good," he admitted nonchalantly though he was secretly savoring every bite. Maybe he had been enjoying manna so much because he had forgotten what "real" food tasted like.

"I was on my way home, in the center of the city, from my parent's house. I was in search of some fresh air from outside the gates. I did not expect anyone to be out here this time of evening." Rahab toyed with the bread in her hands. "And I dare say you are not from this area. What brings you to our city?"

Salmon recognized her curiosity but knew better than to reveal the plans of his people. "My people have been crossing the desert for some time. I was scouting ahead to warn them of any dangers," he admitted truthfully.

"You promised you would not hurt me by witness of 'Jehovah God,' " Rahab repeated. "This is the God you serve?" She asked the question innocently enough, hoping to gain the information she sought, but she was genuinely curious as to the power of this God she had heard about.

"Yes," he answered boldly but kindly, "He is the one true God, the ONLY God," Salmon began. Their conversation continued, Salmon telling her of the wanderings of his people across the desert for the past forty years in search of the land promised to them by their God, and how he had been born during the wanderings knowing no other life. He told her of Moses and the leader he had been, of the parting of the Red Sea which he had only heard about, and their more recent battles against Sihon and Og, which he had been a part of. This man was remarkable, and this God he spoke of was fascinating. Rahab listened intently and realized how passionate and devoted Salmon was to the God of his people. One God. Not several as she was used to her people serving, though she had little use for any of them.

She, in turn, told him of her business with fabrics and of the many gods of her people. He seemed truly interested in her explanations of how she created and dyed her fabrics, and though respectful of her beliefs, asked her questions, not to mock or disrespect her, but questions that truly made her wonder if all she had been taught regarding the gods of her people was accurate. Many of his questions she could not even answer.

She felt genuinely at ease with this man before her, who was no longer so much a stranger, as he was a friend. He made her laugh, he made her think, and he made her feel as if there were more to her than simply the body she possessed. Before she knew it, the sun had begun to sink low in the sky.

"I have enjoyed your stories, and our time together," she admitted. "I have especially enjoyed hearing about the God you serve, but I really must be getting on my way."

"As should I," Salmon agreed as he stood, also unaware of how much time he had spent talking with this woman by whom he was so taken. "Rahab, might I see you again?" He surprised himself by voicing the question aloud.

Rahab looked at him sincerely, a small smile on her lips.

"I thank you, Salmon, for rescuing me, and I appreciate the lovely evening we have spent here, but no. If you really knew me, you would know I am not the type of company your God would approve of you keeping. Our worlds are too far apart." Rahab turned to go but was stopped as he reached out, gently clasping her hand.

"On the contrary, my God is a very forgiving God. He will accept you, regardless of your past, should you choose to turn from your gods and accept Him as your one, true God. As would I," he spoke honestly.

Rahab smiled into the face of this amazing man she had just met. She had no words, but none were needed. She felt sure that she would never see Salmon again after this moment.

Turning again to go, she almost stumbled over the man in the dirt. "I forgot about him," she admitted truthfully.

"I shall tend to him," Salmon assured her. "Get yourself back inside the city and home before darkness falls." Rahab nodded, smiled again, and turned to go. Salmon watched her walk away, wondering as she did so, what she could possibly have meant that would cause him not to want to be in her company.

"I will see you again," Rahab heard him say, but she did not turn again. She continued quickly to the city gates, only realizing when she felt the necklace in the pocket of her tunic that Nazim had not crossed her mind the entire time Salmon was in her presence.

Chapter Six

Her veil securely covering her face once again, Rahab hurried through the gate and back into the streets to the inner courtyard where she could secretly enter her inn. She had allowed herself to think of nothing other than getting home quickly and safely since she had walked away from Salmon. Once she got home, she could reflect on her findings and decide what information she would or would not share with Nazim.

The only thing she could not rid from her mind was the stories of the miracles Salmon's God had performed for His people. Nazim and Jakabed had told her of the crossing of the Red Sea on dry ground and of the battles with the Amorites, but to hear the recollection from Salmon was uncanny. He brought the stories to life. Rahab was not sure her people could withstand an attack from these people should their God command them to fight against them. Yet she was not sure she wanted to give up all of the information she had been so innocently given.

She finally reached her inn and rushed quickly to her chambers. Once there, she pulled the veil from her face and hair and stepped out of the drab tunic she had worn all day. She knew her hair was messy and tattered from the injury she had endured and quickly began heating a basin of water to wash the blood from it. What she had not counted on was the knock on her door.

"Rahab, are you in there?" It was Nazim, and he sounded worried. For a minute she thought of keeping quiet, hoping he would leave but remembered he had let himself in before and could easily do so again should he choose to. Wondering how to avoid too many questions, she wrapped her hair quickly and loosely into a knot to cover the injury at the back of her head and fastened her necklace quickly around her neck. Thankfully the clasp had only come undone and not been broken completely. Nazim pounded at the door again, his voice growing agitated. "Rahab!" he spoke louder.

As she wrapped her robe around her body, she quickly made her way to the door. "No need to be pulling it from the hinges again, Nazim," she smiled as she opened the door.

"Where have you been all day?" he asked, as he strode confidently into the room not waiting to be asked inside. "I have come by twice already," he admitted, as he crossed to the window and pulled the shade as always. She did not miss the frustration in his gait.

"I had to see my parents," she admitted truthfully.

"You are not typically gone for an entire day when you see them. Is everyone well?" he asked, more curious as to what had taken so long than as to the well-being of her family.

Immediately, for reasons she could not put her finger on, she decided against telling him of meeting Salmon. Though at the thought of him, she had to stifle a smile.

"Father was in a talking mood. He and Mother both were actually. He had heard the same rumors you told me of earlier."

Nazim seemed very out of sorts. Uneasy even.

"Are you well, Nazim?" she asked concerned.

"I am. I was just worried for your safety. The king is growing more nervous every day with those Israelites camping on the other side of the river. They seem to be growing restless. I do not want you leaving this inn again until you hear from me."

Rahab knew her brows met her hairline as she straightened her shoulders and looked at Nazim as if he had lost his mind. "You cannot be serious, Nazim," she chuckled, expecting him to do the same.

"On the contrary, I am quite serious," he stated, turning to her, his face a mask of stone.

He quickly realized his mistake in ordering her to stay put by the expression that crossed her features. He sighed deeply and crossed the room to face her directly. He placed his giant hands on her shoulders and looked into her face, just then noticing how tired she looked. "Rahab, I do not mean to order you, but there is a lot going on around the city right now. I do not know if these Israelites are a threat to us or if they will pass around the city wall and leave, but until I am sure of the safety of our people, I would appreciate it if you would just remain here, where I know you are safe." Touching his hand to her chin, he tilted her face toward his and gently kissed the tip of her nose. It was a gentle gesture that he knew she loved, and he hoped it would soften the effect of his words.

He toyed with the pendant on her neck. "I am glad to see you are wearing the pendant. It looks beautiful on you." Rahab looked at how small it seemed when he held it. The biggest mistake she made was looking up into his face again at just that moment. Nazim bent to kiss her lips, and when doing so, he placed his hand at the back of her head. Immediately he withdrew as he felt the dried blood matted in her hair.

He turned her in one swift motion to examine her head, pulling her hair from the knot she had formed. "Rahab, what happened?" he asked in a panicked stupor. She thought quickly, not wanting to divulge everything that had transpired.

"It is nothing, Nazim," she began. "I, I tripped and fell," she tried to lie. He stood before her facing her once again, as if he were frozen, his face a mask of anger. She would hate to be on this man's bad side.

"Where?" he asked firmly, clearly not believing her, "when and where did you trip and fall?"

"On the way back from my parents. I was trying to hurry and lost my balance coming up the steps," she finished quickly.

"Rahab, the blood is dried. You have not been home for very long for I was here just a little while ago, and you were not. Had that just happened, the blood would not be dried." Rahab hated herself for outright lying; she was never good at it. What she was good at, however, was manipulating the truth.

"Tell me what happened, Rahab. The truth this time."

She took a deep breath. "It did happen on the way home from my parents. I had ventured outside the city wall, longing for some solitude. The man you ran from here before attacked me. I was able to escape from him, but not before he knocked me against a palm tree, and I cut my head." There it was out, the truth, well, most of it.

Nazim's jaw was clenched so tightly Rahab was sure he was about to break his teeth. If his concern for her was so intense, why could he not declare his love for her publicly regardless of the consequences? She wondered if he was as protective of her as he was possessive of her.

"He will be dead by morning," Nazim promised and began stalking toward the door. She moved to stand in front of it. She wanted to tell him that the man might be dead already—that a handsome Israelite had swooped in and saved the day, rescuing her and then entertaining her with the miraculous stories of his people's journey in crossing the desert. She wanted to tell him that a God who could perform such miracles could surely use these men to breach the walls of their city, overtake them, and claim their land as their own. She wanted to tell him that this man had made her question everything she had ever believed about the gods they had been taught to serve. That the man, Salmon, had talked to her because he was genuinely interested in her and not just what she could offer him. That he had talked to her without expecting any physical benefits. But she could not tell Nazim any of it. On the contrary, she would not give him any of the information she had obtained from her time with Salmon.

What she would do, however, was keep the two men's paths from crossing. She did not know if Salmon, himself, had made it safely back to camp, but she knew she could not allow Nazim to find Salmon alone in the desert. She did not know for which man she would fear for the most. What a battle that would be, she realized.

Thinking quickly, she went with the one tactic she knew would work. "Do not leave me this night, Nazim," she begged softly. "Wait until morning. Help me clean my wound and stay with me." She had never asked him to stay the night before. She knew it admitted dependence on him, but she had to keep him out of the desert for at least a little while. The risk was too great to allow him to leave.

Nazim bent to kiss her, and she recognized the passion in the kiss. He lifted her effortlessly and carried her toward the bathing tub. She had secured him for the night, but for the first time in her life, she wondered over the decision she had made and over the task she was about to perform. She was sure that Salmon's God would not approve.

Salmon sat at the fireside again with both Joshua and Caleb. He had been much closer to the wall today and had drawn his description in the dirt as they discussed their strategy. "The city looks to be surrounded by a great mound of earth with a stone wall at the base," he explained. "The outer retaining wall must be close to fifteen feet high with a mud-brick wall at least twenty-five feet high resting at the top of it. It almost appears as if a second wall rests beyond the outer one. It will be humanly impossible for us to destroy that outer wall alone, much less whatever barricades they have inside it," he explained.

"Our God has never been one to take the easy way out," Joshua admitted.

"Though he will provide a way," Caleb reminded them.

"Once Garrick and I get inside that outer wall, we should be able to see exactly what other fortresses, if any, lie beyond it."

Salmon continued briefly telling them of the maiden he had met. And though he had gained little information from her, he had made sure she had plenty of information to report back to her people on the God they serve and the miracles He had performed on their behalf.

This time Garrick had joined them, as eager as Salmon to enter inside the city walls to see what information they would be able to obtain. They would leave tonight; using the shallowest spot in the river to cross as Salmon had done twice now. Posing as traveling merchants, they would enter at dawn. They would return to camp within three days time to report back to Joshua. With their plan in action and their prayers lifted, the men departed under cover of darkness.

Chapter Seven

"Rahab, I have a confession to make," Nazim began several hours later. They lay side by side, facing one another. Rahab smoothed the hair from his forehead. "For the first time in my life of service to the king," he began, "I can honestly say he is afraid," he paused then continued. "As are most of my men."

"Of the Israelites?" she questioned, already knowing his answer.

"Of the Israelites," he confirmed. "They are not a very big army to have accomplished such amazing feats. Yet, their determination and solidarity are uncanny."

Rahab propped on her elbow. Though they were close, Nazim rarely confided in her this way. "Tell me more of this God they serve, Nazim." She wanted to know exactly what he knew.

Nazim turned to his back, his eyes never leaving the ceiling as he spoke. "There is little I know about Him other than the stories I have already told you," he began, being completely open and honest with her. "The king is concerned about the Red Sea crossing, and that happened over forty years ago. He is afraid this God they speak of has grown even greater in power since that time. But I am more in awe of their recent victory in defeating the Amorites. Regardless of which story captivates you the most, the feats are comparable. Their God seems to be using them to achieve almost anything. He seems invincible."

"Nazim, do you ever feel that there really could be just one god? What if theirs is the only true God? What if all the gods we pray to are nothing more than figments of our imagination."

"I do not claim to be a scholar on religion, Rahab," he admitted, turning his head to look at her. "I am a man of battle, not a man of spirituality. Yet, I do not have a reason to scoff at the gods of our nation and render them useless. Especially just because of stories and rumors I have heard."

"You just admitted that even the king himself is fearful of these Israelites and of the God they serve."

"Yes, I did admit that their God is powerful and is using them in mighty ways," he clarified, "but I did not say that our gods could not do a mighty work in us as well." He spoke the words convincingly, but Rahab was not certain he had even convinced himself of that.

"I have not seen our gods performing any miracles, Nazim," she spoke truthfully. "I only see people praying and sacrificing to stone idols that are set up in the temple, idols that can be knocked over or stolen or moved from place to place. This God they speak of is not a piece of stone that can be handled or manipulated."

Nazim lay still for a moment, gazing again at the ceiling, seemingly lost in thought. "I know not of their God, nor very much of our gods if the truth be told," he admitted finally, "and I suppose if their God is behind their victories as they proclaim He is then we all should be a bit unnerved by His power." He lay in silence for a moment, and Rahab gave him time to collect his thoughts. When he finally broke the silence, she knew the subject was closed. "I just do not know," he sighed, "but what I do know," he continued, turning to face her and pull her into his arms "is that I need to get some sleep. I have a man to kill tomorrow and perhaps a few Israelites while I am at it." She settled against him knowing there was a grin on his face as he kissed the top of her head.

Rahab lay against him as his breathing became even and steady. Just a few days ago she would have felt secure, protected, and perfectly content with what she had at this moment, nestled in his strong arms with perhaps a glimmer of hope that perhaps one day there could be a future for them together. Yet tonight, her thoughts wandered, not to the man who lay with her now and held her, but to the man who had rescued her just a few hours before.

Salmon poked his head from above the water. The river had begun to swell, signaling the warm spring days had thawed the snow and ice from the mountains above them—a sure sign this river would continue to deepen. He glanced over his shoulder as Garrick came up behind him snorting and coughing. "So much for being stealthy at the moment," he chuckled under his breath. Luckily there was not a soul nearby to hear him.

"How under the heavens will we ever get our entire militia across this river, much less over that wall?" Garrick asked as he pulled himself onto the bank.

"As Caleb often reminds us, God will provide a way," Salmon reminded him from his place on the shore. "And as Joshua often states, God never takes the easy way out." He began to remove his sandals. "Do not forget how Moses began this journey by leading everyone across the Red Sea. We just need to concern ourselves with getting inside those gates for now. I feel we are close enough to camp here for the night and go in at first light. That is when traveling merchants will be entering the city, and we should be able to enter then without too much speculation."

Salmon made a place for himself on the ground under a tree and gazed at the stars above. He was quiet in his musings when Garrick broke the silence from his own place on the ground.

"So...about this maiden you mentioned earlier," he began, and Salmon caught the laughter in his voice.

Salmon smiled in the darkness. Yes, he had thought of her often tonight since they had left camp for the city and was secretly hoping to run into her again, yet at the same time, somewhat afraid he would. It would not bode well if she recognized him inside the city. Too, he also feared she was correct that their worlds were too far apart. That did not change the fact, however, that she was a beauty, and her spirit seemed as sweet as her fragrance.

"Do not concern yourself with my affairs," he finally spoke to Garrick with a grin. "You sound like a little girl," he scoffed.

Garrick respected Salmon enough to let the conversation lag. He did not intend to pry beyond the attempt he had already made. It was Salmon who broke the silence next.

"She is a seamstress. With raven black hair and eyes as deep as the sea," he began. Garrick snorted with laughter. Salmon threw a twig in his direction. "Now go to sleep," he commanded playfully. "I shall keep the first watch."

As Rahab expected, before the sun rose the next morning, Nazim was gone. A handful of coins lay on the pillow where his head had been. It was an unintentional reminder of what their relationship really was. She did not hurry to move from her place but instead lay in thought.

Thoughts of Salmon had filled her dreams during the night, and though she would not deny he was captivatingly handsome, it was the stories of his God that she could not get away from. He had told her that his God was a forgiving One who would accept her should she choose to serve Him. But Salmon did not really know her. He did not know the profession she had chosen. How could he be so sure that His God was forgiving enough to accept a harlot into His presence?

She thought of the gods she had been taught to worship as a child. She had never understood the way her people sacrificed their animals, and sometimes even their children, before an idol they had created from clay and stone themselves. She had partaken in the rituals as a child but had forsaken the practice, taking no part in it since she had left her parent's house and started her life with Nariman so many years ago. Even the gods her people served would frown on a profession such as hers.

Rahab turned to her back to stare at the ceiling and then quickly back to her side when the back of her head hit the pillow. The soreness reminded her how differently her life could have been. If Salmon had not arrived when he did yesterday, would she have been alive today? A thought flitted into her mind. Could his God have been protecting her even then? How many times over the years had even Nazim arrived at just the right moment? Was Salmon's God watching over her even in the life she had been living?

She lay there for what seemed like an hour reliving the stories that Salmon had shared with her, her mind flitting back and forth from the past to the present. She recounted instances in her own life where it seemed something, or someone, had protected her from circumstances that could have ended so differently. She thought of Nariman and the pain and fear she showed when dying. Salmon did not speak of the battles and wanderings their people had endured with fear because he trusted in the God he served.

How refreshing it had been to have a conversation with someone, especially a man, who did not simply talk with her to ease his own conscience of the activities they were about to or had just engaged in, and even those conversations were few and far between. Salmon showed little interest in her physical attributes at all. Besides her parents, Nazim was the only person she ever had a real conversation with, and primarily even his visits were for another purpose.

And what about Nazim? Nazim, who had always been such a force of nature himself, seemed fearful when he spoke of the God of the camp of the Israelites. Rahab knew Nazim had said their conversation last night was about the king's fear, but she knew the true fear stemmed from Nazim himself. He would never outright admit it, but their conversation had been more about him than the king.

A beam of sunlight filtered through her window and across the cot where she lay. It was almost as if something, or someone, were reaching out to her. She placed her hand in the beam and watched as her fingers danced in the light. Her entire life had been lived in darkness. She had to cover herself completely and dance in and out of shadows when she went out. Men would slip in and out of her inn under cover of night so as not to be seen. Her fabrics were sold to merchants who bought from her in secret, and those who wore her garments had no idea it was she who had dyed and created them.

Rahab rose so quickly from the cot that she barely heard the sound of Nazim's coins hit the floor or the feeling of her head as it began to spin. She wanted to know more about this God of Salmon — a God who cared for and protected His people yet was powerful enough to strike fear in the hearts of men like Nazim and the king. She longed to leave the darkness behind. She wanted to step out of the shadows and be proud of the garments she dyed and created. She longed to talk to people, to women and children, and to have real conversations about the lives they lived. She wanted to openly share her garments with others and be proud of the work she created.

Somehow, she would find Salmon again and ask him the questions she had that had so long gone unanswered. She was tired of living a life that had to be lived in the shadows, tired of a profession she was ashamed of, and so tired of being nothing more than a harlot. She longed to be free. Yet, the sad fact loomed about in her mind as she now held her head in her hands and began to cry. Would she ever be?

Chapter Eight

Salmon and Garrick pulled their cloaks over their heads as they approached the city wall. A large band of traveling merchants was about to enter the gates, and the plan was to join the caravan inconspicuously near the end and then separate themselves from them once inside the city. The leader of the group gave the signal after talking with the gatekeeper, and the entire company began to move beyond the wall, completely unaware of the two men who fell into place among them.

Salmon had taken his place at the very back of the caravan with Garrick mingling in about halfway through. Salmon watched as Garrick entered the city, he himself not far behind. He was glad he had chosen Garrick to come with him. Although young, he was mature for his age. He walked right past the guard, unnoticed, as Salmon himself was about to do.

Salmon had been correct about a second wall that now loomed above them. Homes and business were built into the walls themselves. Attempting to take it in without being obvious, he noticed the second wall had no retaining wall below it but rested on the crest of the embankment that rose up from the outer wall. The city was well fortified by the earth itself, let alone the two walls built against it, at least six foot thick each.

"Our God never takes the easy way out," he remembered Joshua saying once again. Joshua did not know how right he had been. Salmon could not see an easy way out this time, for certain.

They were now safely inside the inner-city wall, and Salmon noticed that Garrick had begun falling back from the caravan. He watched as the young man bent as if to adjust the straps of his sandal, allowing others to pass and giving Salmon time to catch up to him. Once they were in close proximity, Garrick took the opportunity to dart into an alleyway with Salmon close behind. The men ducked into the shadows and hid themselves completely while still being able to view the main street.

"You were right about the wall having two parts, Salmon," Garrick began in a hushed whisper. "They will be impossible to breach."

"Nothing is impossible with God," Salmon reminded him as he continued to watch the street from where they came. "Did you notice the centurions patrolling these streets?" he asked, pointing to a dark-haired man as big as himself. "It seems as if they have as much trouble within as they are about to have without," Salmon continued.

"Or that they are expecting trouble," Garrick concluded.

Salmon nodded. "By all the activity on the rooftops, they have to know we are camping across the Jordan. No doubt they have heard of our victories. We need to see the layout of the city and find the palace," Salmon continued with his instructions. "Be cautious, I do not like the looks of their soldiers. Especially," he paused, pointing across the street to where Nazim stood watch, "that one. He seems especially tense, and there must be a reason for it." Garrick nodded in understanding. "Let's go," Salmon finished.

Garrick stepped aside and motioned to the street beyond them.

"You first," he grinned.

Nazim tightened the leather strap that held his hair firmly at the back of his head. He could not ease the nagging feeling that something was about to happen. Last night's conversation with Rahab about their enemies and the powerful God they served had kept him from resting even after Rahab had slept, though he noticed that even her sleep had been less than peaceful. He wondered if her restlessness stemmed from the conversation they had shared concerning gods or if he himself caused her tension.

He knew their "relationship" was different than the others that she entertained. She would love nothing more than for him to declare his love for her publicly but to do so would bring him ruin. He had worked for years for his place in the militia. Chief centurion to the king was not a position to be taken lightly, and it was not something he was willing to give up even for Rahab. He had offered to take care of her privately if she would allow him the privilege of being her only guest, but she was not willing to be solely dependent on him. Yet how would it be any different if he took her to wife? Would she not be solely dependent on him them?

"*Women!*" He thought exasperated as he pinched the corners of his eyes. He hated himself for becoming so emotionally involved with a woman who traded sex for money. She honestly meant more to him than she realized and truthfully probably even more than he himself realized. His attachment to her was as mental as it was physical, but no one else could ever know. And now all this talk of gods and Israelites and coming wars… he shook his head to clear it. Thankfully he was able to easily maintain his outer composure, masking his inner turmoil.

He took a deep breath and laid his head against the wall, appearing only remotely interested in his surroundings. Yet his mind continued to work frantically as he stood watch. He had to remain rational where Rahab was concerned. His relationship or attachment, whatever it was, with her would have to be worked through later. He was a warrior, and his first duty was to protect this land and his king. It was just the fear of the unknown that had him so unsettled, he thought. He needed answers.

How did an army of wandering slaves rise to defeat so many neighboring cities, including the Amorites? Regardless of the God they served, there had to be more to it. More battle strategies, more planning, something to enable them to continuously claim victory. There was only one way to know. He would ask. He would travel across the river to Gilead, the land of the Amorites. Once there, he would find someone who had witnessed these Israelites in action, someone with more information about their warriors and their God. He would then return to Jericho, knowing exactly how to defeat them should the need arise. Or perhaps, just to be rid of them.

Devising a plan was easy, he loved a good battle strategy, and yet carrying it out with the city under full alert would be another issue. The trip there and back would take him a full week at the least, and that was only if he was able to find the information he sought quickly.

As his mind worked formulating an idea to carry out his plan, a young traveler caught his eye. The man had come in with a large caravan of merchants, nothing unusual about that, but it was when he paused to tighten the laces of his sandals that Nazim thought his actions rather odd. He looked innocent enough as he continued to hold his bent position allowing others to pass, but Nazim noticed that his task was completed well before he rose. He continued to toy with his laces, glancing over his shoulder as he did so.

It wasn't until another man approached that he moved, and then both of them disappeared into a nearby alleyway. Nazim continued to maintain his position against the wall while slowly looking back and forth. If they had noticed him, he did not want them to realize that he too had taken notice of them. A moment passed before both men emerged and continued down the street together.

Nazim watched them weave through the crowd and saw his second in command, Jenoah, nearby. He whistled just loud enough for the man to hear him and with a nod of his head, motioned for him to come. Jenoah moved quickly across the street to his captain.

"Do those two men there seem familiar at all?" he asked, pointing discreetly to the backs of Garrick and Salmon.

"No, sir," Jenoah answered. "They came through the gates with a large group of travelers. However, they seemed to have gotten separated," he admitted, straining his neck to see through the crowd.

"Do not cause any attention, but something does not sit well with me concerning those two. I want to know who they are and what they are doing here," Nazim commanded.

He began to walk in the direction they had gone. They must have moved quickly, for now, he could not lay his eyes on them. Jenoah had kept a steady pace several feet behind him so no one would pay attention to the fact that something alarming had caught the eye of his Captain.

Rahab stood on her rooftop, stretching her back. Her quest for answers regarding Salmon and his God would have to wait. There was so much work that went into transforming flax into linens, even after the arduous task of harvesting was done. Once harvesting was complete, the flax must be allowed to dry, and then it must be scutched, or beaten, and then hackled. Finally, after weeks of preparation and work, she would see the fine fibers she longed for.

Her flax had been drying for several days, and it was now time to flip the reeds so the backside could dry as well. Half of her harvest had been turned. In truth, this process was almost as difficult as the harvesting. The reeds were heavy and awkward, and the smell very unpleasant. She had been fortunate to have a good harvest, and her rooftop was full of the fruits of her labor. Still, there was much more to be done, and she did not want to waste such a warm day. It was a perfect day for the drying process.

Continuing to stretch her back before beginning to turn the second half of the reeds, a rapid movement from inside the city caught her eye. It was doubtful anyone from the ground below would have noticed, but from her vantage point on the rooftop, it was plain to see. Nazim had been propped casually against the wall as he watched the streets. She could spot him easily. Then suddenly he had pushed from the wall and begun a steady walk through the streets, dodging people as he went. She searched the crowd ahead and noticed two men who seemed to stand out from the others. Hoods covered their heads and faces, and their tunics were a different shade of brown from what most of their city owned.

A disturbing thought occurred to Rahab, and she bolted to the other side of her rooftop to look over the Jordan River where the Israelites were camped. She knew fabrics, and she knew colors, and what she saw was exactly what she had expected and what she had feared. The two men Nazim was after were travelers from the Israelite camp. They had entered the city! If Nazim caught up to them and realized from where they came, he would have no mercy.

Quickly she ran down the steps of the roof and into the inn, down the inside steps, and into the outer courtyard. There was no time to be as subtle as she would like to be, but if Nazim caught up to them before she did, there would be no hope. She ran through the corridors, down the alleyway and up to the stone wall; the same stone wall from where she had spied on Nariman so many years ago.

She looked quickly through the openings, searching for something. Her view was so much better from the roof! Wait, there! She spotted them, paused at a merchant's table trying to look as if they were inquiring to the wares of the seller. She waited for them to move closer, hoping they would do so quickly. Finally, they turned, heading in her direction. One of the men looked her way, and she could not believe the face she recognized beneath the hood. It was Salmon!

Quickly moving to the end of the stone wall, she knew she only had one chance. If they changed their course or moved to the center of the street, she would never be able to get their attention. The minutes seemed like hours as they slowly continued to advance in her direction. Finally, they were in close proximity, and she knew this was her only chance.

"Salmon," she spoke through the opening in a loud whisper just as his ear passed by her hiding place. He paused and looked around just long enough for her to reach around the edge of the wall, grab the sleeve of his tunic and pull him into her hiding place.

Garrick stopped completely, turning this way and that attempting to figure out to where his friend had vanished.

"Rahab?" he heard Salmon exclaim and looked around the wall now behind him to where his companion had disappeared. Rahab felt her cheeks flush for the first time in years, as Salmon took in her attire.

"There's no time to explain here," she commanded softly yet fervently, "you must come with me."

Chapter Nine

Rahab moved swiftly through the corridors and alleyway, making her way up the stairs and into her inn, Salmon and Garrick close behind her. Once they were safely inside her rooms, she turned to catch her breath, locking the door firmly behind them.

"There is little time to explain," she began, "I feel you are safe here but only for a time. We will not have long before Nazim seeks you out."

"I take it being a seamstress is not your only profession," Salmon stated coldly, stopping her in her tracks. She slowly turned to look at him, and for the first time in more years than she could remember, Rahab was embarrassed at her appearance; her midriff exposed and top cut low, her long thick braid draped over her shoulder while her legs were barely hidden by the thin fabric covering them. Garrick, having never seen a woman in such little attire, was every shade of red. In truth, neither had Salmon, though he was much better at controlling his features.

"Perhaps we should leave," he finished, when she remained silent, and he moved to open the door now behind her.

"My profession is not important right now," she stammered as she quickly recovered and moved to block the door. "Despite what you think of me at the moment, you must follow me for the sake of your own lives. If Nazim catches up to the two of you, there will be no need for explanations from anyone, and we have little time." Quickly she moved to the stairs leading to the rooftop.

The men looked at one another in question as Rahab began to mount the stairs, realizing this was not an establishment they should be in. She stopped when she realized they failed to follow her.

"Please," she urged while looking into Salmon's face. "Trust me. I have witnessed his pursuit of you," she pleaded. "You cannot afford to be found."

Salmon turned again to Garrick as unspoken approval crossed the younger man's features.

"If we are being followed, a harlot's chambers is not the first place they would think to look for Israelites," Garrick stated quietly, shrugging his shoulders. Salmon thought for a moment and realized his companion was right.

The men began to follow Rahab up the steep steps though not as quickly as she would have liked. It was painfully obvious to her that they were still reluctant and very uncomfortable at being in the inn of a harlot.

At last, they reached the rooftop, which remained covered in the large stalks of flax she had spent all day turning. Rahab motioned for them to stay low, worried that their height may allow them to be seen by anyone looking up from below. As the men crouched in the center of her roof, she moved to the edge overlooking the city, searching for signs of Nazim or other soldiers who had been alerted to keep an eye out for the spies.

Finally, she saw Nazim well past the entrance of her inn. His pace had slowed, but it was obvious he continued on full alert. Rahab motioned for her guests to join her quietly, and as they did so, she spoke to them in clear but low tones.

"There," she said, pointing him out. "He is the chief centurion to the king. I saw him trailing you. He will find you, Salmon, if you do not allow me to help you get out of the city." Rahab's eyes seemed to burn into his soul. He knew she was desperate to help him.

She turned to leave him with his thoughts and moved to begin clearing a section of the roof in the middle of the large stalks of flax. Her arms, already tired from turning the stalks all day, burned from her efforts. The men continued to take in the city from this viewpoint. From here they had a clear view of the layout, including the location of the palace. Once they had taken it all in, they looked one to another before moving to assist her. Salmon was not sure what she was doing, but followed her lead, continuing to aid her until she stopped.

Garrick paused to look over the other side of the rooftop facing the Jordan River and their campsite.

"How long have you been watching us?" he asked, turning to Rahab as he realized how clearly he could see their camp from this spot. Salmon had joined him and was wondering the same thing.

"Since the day you made camp," she answered truthfully, "and I am not the only one who has noticed you. All of our men are talking of the Israelites who have camped on the other side of the river, and they wonder as to your business there".

"I have told you our business," Salmon spoke plainly. "We are in search of our Promised Land."

"But I have not told them," she answered equally as plain, "although we have heard." She could tell by the tone of his voice that he was unhappy at his discovery of her. "Salmon, I can only imagine what you must think of me," she admitted painfully. "But regardless of your thoughts, I never told you anything that was not true. We met but once, and in that time I may have withheld information from you, but nothing I said to you was inaccurate in any way. I daresay you withheld information from me as well, lest you would not have sneaked inside our gates." He had to agree with her on that one. She had told him their worlds were far apart, and she had told him his God would not approve of their keeping company. He had to give her credit for being honest. "And for what it is worth, I never spoke of our meeting to anyone," she promised him, breaking the silence.

"Why did you not?" he asked, sincerely curious.

"Because for one, they have heard enough. Currently, my people can only speculate as to the reasons you may be keeping so close to our city. I did not want to alarm them more by confirming that you search for your "Promised Land" as they have been told, or that our land is a part of that land and that your people plan to claim it as their own. Besides, our city is well secured as you have now seen for yourself. I have no trouble believing your God can do miraculous things," she assured him, "but you now have proof that our walls are nearly impassable unless we allow you to come in. And you have seen our centurions," she finished with surety.

Salmon laughed at how serious she was. "We will have no trouble with your walls or your centurions," he promised her. "I do not know when and how it will come to pass, Rahab, but I can assure you, we will take your city for it is the land that was promised to us by Jehovah God." He saw surprise cross her features and instantly recognized he was being too confident in his own abilities. "Let me rephrase that," he continued humbly. "By the grace of God, we will overtake your city," he spoke slowly and then dropped his head immediately asking God to forgive him of his arrogance.

"What are you doing?" she asked instantly. When he was finished with his quick prayer, he looked to her.

"I was asking Jehovah God to forgive me for my arrogance. I do not know His plan, Rahab, but I do know that He keeps His promises. And Jericho is part of the land He has promised to us. However, the tone and the conceited way in which I spoke to you made it seem as if I could overtake your city on my own. Our strength comes from God alone, and without Him, we can do nothing. I apologize for insulting your fortresses as well."

"You are not in a temple, much less in front of an idol, and yet you pray?" Rahab was clearly in awe of such a God who could hear prayers from any location.

"My God is not an idol, as I told you before," he clarified. "Rahab, our God is with us always and is in control of every situation. We are free to call out to Him at any time."

"And He will forgive you at your request just that simply? Just by you bowing your head and praying to him?"

"If done so sincerely, then yes. I told you, He is a very forgiving God," he explained again.

Rahab hated herself for allowing it, but she felt a tear roll along her cheek. She could not shake this feeling of conviction and regret. Quickly she turned away.

"He will forgive you as well, Rahab, should you choose to turn away from your life here and ask Him to," Salmon spoke quietly as he moved to come up behind her. He placed his hands on her shoulders, turning her to face him. "You need only repent and declare Him as your God."

"I have thought of little else since our meeting outside the wall," she admitted though her voice quivered. "I just do not know how I can turn from this life I have created, and from," she paused, reluctant to say Nazim. Instead, she finished with, "my people."

An immense pounding from the street below interrupted them. Rahab rushed to the edge of the rooftop and looked down, her heart thundering inside her chest. Jakabed was at her door.

"Rahab," he called. "Show yourself, harlot!" At those words, she knew his visit was not for the sake of entertainment. He was here looking for the Israelites, and he wanted anyone in listening distance to know it.

"Stay here and do not come down those stairs," she commanded Salmon. "No matter what."

With that, she ran down the steps and to the door where Jakabed had begun to grow impatient. She wiped her face, smiled, as she was accustomed to doing, and opened the door quickly.

"Jakabed," she exclaimed cheerfully. "Today is not your regular day to visit."

Jakabed smiled at her recognition of him as being such a loyal customer. He was clearly comfortable with visiting her regularly, regardless of who knew it, a true mark of his character.

"I am not here to visit you," he admitted truthfully, "for the moment," he finished smugly. "I am here seeking information." She stood at the door refusing him entrance but noticing how he continued to look past her into her inn. "We are searching for intruders within our city. Have you seen them?"

Rahab shook her head. "I have been inside all day and have not ventured outside this inn," she knew she was no good at lying, but that was not entirely a lie. She had been within the boundaries of her inn all day. It was enough.

"Very well," he spoke loudly, "but if you are visited by two men who are not from here, you must notify the palace immediately," he commanded.

"Now, Jakabed, you know I keep my customers' identities quiet. And, besides, if these Israelites have come into our city, do you really think my inn is a place they would visit?" She laughed, causing the stocky man to laugh with her.

"I suppose you are right, but nonetheless." He turned to go but not before giving her playful pop on the rear. "I will see you very soon," he promised as he stalked away. Oh, how he repulsed her, she thought as she watched him strut away.

Quickly she ran back up the steps. If Jakabed returned to Nazim and bragged about speaking to her as she expected he would, Nazim was sure to follow up very soon. She had to get Salmon and Garrick hidden.

As she again approached the rooftop, she realized the men had heard the entire exchange below.

"Please tell me that disgusting little man is not the man who gave you that pendant," Salmon spoke as she approached.

"No, he is not," she spoke confidently. "But he is one who will be enough to bring attention to the fact that you 'are not' here, if you follow me."

Garrick looked back and forth between them. "I do not follow you," he admitted.

"She means that he will tell others that he was here, bringing attention to the fact that we could be, even though she said we are not," Salmon clarified slowly.

"Exactly," Rahab confirmed.

Garrick still seemed puzzled, but the conversation continued, nonetheless.

"The two of you must remain extremely quiet and not move from this rooftop for as long as it takes me to help you get to safety. Salmon, I will be completely honest with you from this point on," she promised. "I do not know if I can change my life, there is still more about me that you do not know."

"Regarding the 'not betrothed, but dear friend' who gave you that pendant I presume?" he interrupted, pointing to the pendant ever-present on her chest and referring to the conversation they had when they first met.

"Yes," she admitted, her fingers going to the pendant lying there. "I do not know my fate in all of this, but I cannot shake the conviction that all you say is true when you tell me that the Lord has given you this land. I told you that my people have been speculating as to why you have been camped across the river. We are not simpletons, Salmon. We have heard how the Lord dried up the Red Sea for you when you fled from Egypt. We have heard how you utterly destroyed the two kings of the Amorites at Sihon and Og. Our men had been told of these rumors, long before you and I met, and they tremble in fear because of the miracles your God has performed on your behalf."

She stood tall and looked both of the men before her straight in the face as she continued. "I believe all you have told me, and I believe that the Lord your God, He is God in heaven above, and in earth beneath. Please, I pray you, swear unto me by the Lord since I have shown you kindness that you will also show kindness to my family and to me," she pleaded thinking of her parents, brothers, and sister. "Please deliver us from the death and destruction that is about to come to our city." Rahab did not hide the tears that escaped from her eyes and ran along her face.

"As Jehovah God is my witness, we will do you no harm," Salmon promised her for the second time since she had first met him. "We will find a way to keep you and your family safe."

With a nod of agreement and confirmation from Garrick, the trio once again went to work.

Nazim continued his search for the strangers, determined to find them before night fell. Few he asked had even noticed them. The few who had spoken with them claimed they were just inquisitive as to things such as the location of the palace and the best place in town for food and beverage. Jenoah had reported on one occasion that they had been seen looking at wares at one of the same merchants' tables with whom who they had entered the city. That was odd. Why would they be looking to purchase from the very people they were supposedly in the company of? It was a question that once he caught up to them, he would surely ask.

Where and how had they disappeared? Nazim had been all over the city with no sign of them for hours, yet he was certain they had not left through the gates.

The sun had just begun to set when Jenoah approached Nazim propped against the wall at his favorite spot to observe the streets.

"No sign, captain," he spoke as he approached. "It is as if they have vanished."

"They are here somewhere," Nazim spoke slow and sure, his eyes never leaving the street in front of him. Jenoah watched as his leader's jaw clenched and released, a sure sign of his intensive anger.

"Jakabed was rambling to some of the other officers of 'his connections' within the city," Jenoah scoffed, trying to lighten his captain's mood. "The imbecile even bragged that he had visited the harlot to see if they had shown up in her quarters. He said that she told him she had been inside all day, just waiting for him to come to visit her," Jenoah mocked in a high-pitched voice. He was expecting Nazim to at least smile but was met with a face of cold stone. "Jakabed is so proud of the fact that he is well-known to her," he continued, "that he forgets how ridiculous it makes him look that he is a regular visitor to the city whore," he finished with a laugh. He cleared his throat awkwardly when he failed to receive the reaction he had anticipated from his leader.

Nazim held himself in check, rejecting his desire to pelt the man in front of him into the earth, knowing to do so would make him look equally as ridiculous as Jakabed. Yet, he now had a sure sign he could share with no one the relationship he had with Rahab. Just before, he had almost convinced himself to share his dilemma with this, his most trusted friend, the same friend who had just voiced his opinion unknowingly.

Rahab was so much more to him, but she would never be anything more than a harlot to the people who mattered. He reminded himself that to admit his affections for her would surely cause him to lose all the respect and admiration he had gained in his years of service to the king, as well as the position he now held.

He had just begun to scan the street again when a thought occurred to him. The idea burned in his chest, causing his face to turn different shades of red as he continued to process the thought. His breathing became slow and deep as the realization continued to form in his mind. He could not believe the ridiculous, yet quite possible scenario that had come to him.

All the questions Rahab had asked him the last time they were together, the interest she had expressed in the God of the Israelites, the topics they had discussed. Nazim thought back over that conversation, putting everything into perspective. Now, it almost seemed to him as if Rahab were on the side of their enemies. By the time full realization finally hit his mind, he was seething in anger. His fingers went to his forehead as he came to grips with the conclusion he had come to. With his head spinning, he looked to the building directly in front of him. Quite possible, and even more probable, the location of the intruders had been within his view the majority of the day, and he had been too blind to see it.

"Captain?" Jenoah questioned astounded at the sudden change in Nazim's features. "Captain, what is it?" he asked, alarmed at his leader's sudden motion.

"Stay here," he commanded sternly as he lurched forward in the direction of Rahab's inn, his face a mask of stone and his hand firmly grasping the hilt of his sword. Jenoah shuddered unsure of what was happening but also fearful of ever finding himself on the wrong side of Nazim.

Chapter Ten

The plan Rahab developed and shared with Salmon and Garrick would not be perfect, but with the help of God in Heaven, it would keep the spies safe. The two men would hide on the rooftop; covered by the large stalks of flax that Rahab had drying there. The reeds would be heavy, smelly, and uncomfortable, but the men would be well hidden. Once darkness had completely fallen, Rahab would return to the rooftop, uncover them and let them down from her window. There they could scale the outer city wall facing the Jordan where they could then escape the city under cover of complete and total darkness.

The men lay side by side to fit into the space Rahab had prepared. She had no way of knowing how long they would have to stay hidden, so she urged them to lay as comfortably as possible.

As she worked to cover them, they talked quietly. They told her more of their God and stories of great men and great battles that had come before them. They spoke to her of forgiveness and sanctification.

She continued working but took in everything they said, asking questions, and gaining the answers she sought. They talked and worked well into the evening before she finally felt secure in their hiding place, and secure in her decision to follow their God.

She was completely focused on her work, determined to keep them safe, and faltered only when Salmon reached up from his position, grabbing her hand in his own.

"I promise we will not forget your kindness, Rahab," he assured her. "We do not take the danger you place yourself in lightly. Your protection of us will forever be remembered, and God will reward you for your goodness to us, as will we."

"Do not thank me yet," she joked. "Nazim is a stubborn man, and he will search this inn from top to bottom if he feels the need."

"Nazim?" Salmon questioned as understanding dawned, remembering the man she had pointed out to him earlier. "He is the man who gave you that pendant? The 'dear friend to whom you are *not* betrothed?'" She recognized the statement he had hidden in the question.

Rahab looked to the pendant resting on her chest. "He is," she admitted, and he caught the moment of confusion that crossed her face as she toyed with the pendant with her free hand.

Rahab's breath caught in her throat when Salmon gently kissed the hand he had continued to hold.

"I have complete confidence in our God to keep us safe from anything, or anyone, which you cannot," he assured her holding her hand a moment more.

Rahab paused only a moment before she gently pulled her hand from his grasp and began her work once again. Fairly quickly, she had the men completely covered in the reeds, making sure there was no visible sign that anything other than flax was laying on her rooftop. She was glad that she had made a mental note as to where the men were hidden, lest she herself would lose track of exactly where she had made their hiding place, especially once night had completely fallen. Satisfied with her work, she bent to remind them once more not to move or to speak until she gave them word and began the process of uncovering them. With their promise, she made her way back inside.

Her heart was troubled. Salmon stirred some emotion within her. He had kissed her hand so tenderly; almost as if he cherished her hand as he held it. Nazim had shown her tenderness before, but with Salmon, it seemed different somehow. Salmon seemed to enjoy her company without the promise or pretense of anything more than a simple conversation. Her relationship with Nazim had been built upon physical attraction, and though, through the years they had formed an emotional attachment, very seldom did his visits not end with his physical desires being met.

Nazim! His name coming to her mind, brought her back to her current state of reality. Rahab shook her head to clear it. She had no time to focus on anything right now other than protecting the men in her care and helping them to escape to freedom. With the city now descending into darkness, she had a strong feeling that time was approaching.

She began rummaging through baskets and bags of fabrics looking for something strong enough to safely allow the men to climb down the outer wall. They were not small men; Salmon was every bit as large as Nazim, though Garrick was of a somewhat smaller stature. Just anything would not be able to hold their weight as they climbed down the wall.

Finally, the perfect item came to mind, and she crossed the room to grab it without a second thought. The scarlet she had been saving for a "special occasion." She was certain she would never have an occasion in her life as special as this one, especially if it meant getting the Israelites to safety. She pulled the scarlet fabric from where she had stored it and began twisting the pieces together to form an unbreakable cord. She knew the piece may become tattered beyond use, but nothing would ever be as important to her as this moment. Tying it off at the bottom, she had almost convinced herself to return to the roof, uncover the men and help them escape when she heard the familiar, yet much more aggressive than usual, voice coming from outside in the street.

"RAHAB!" Nazim thundered just before he began his assault on the door. "Open this door this instant, or I shall do so!" he yelled, his fist never stopping his brutal assault on the closed portal.

Rahab paused for only a second as she took the handle, closed her eyes, and uttered a desperate plea to the God she had chosen to serve. "Please, help me keep Your men safe, no matter the consequences," she whispered. She knew she was about to put on the show of her life.

Pulling open the door, she looked completely astounded as to why Nazim was being so forceful.

"Nazim," she began as if totally confused, "why the urgency?" She barely had the door open before he pushed his way past her, almost knocking her down.

"Where are they?" he stormed as he began walking quickly from room to room looking inside each one and behind every door. He was certain he would find them hiding somewhere within.

"Where are who?" she asked, rather impatiently, her hand still on the open door. "And you do realize you entered my inn from the city entrance?" she began, though he paid no attention to her question. She had seen him angry before, but never in such a rage.

"Rahab, two Israelites have been seen within our city, and I want to know what business they have here. Tell me, do you know of them?" Nazim's breathing was heavy, and never before had she seen his face so flushed. He never paused in his search, and she almost slammed the door in her haste to follow after him when he approached the stairs to the rooftop and took them by twos.

"Oh God," she prayed silently as he approached the rooftop ahead of her. Rahab stood by the steps in silent alarm as he stalked around the edge of the roof, trying to look casual as she possibly could. "Nazim, what are you searching for?" she asked as he kicked through the reeds directly in front of him. She had to distract him from continuing his search through the reeds. "You know you are ruining all my hard work," she criticized.

"I saw them, Rahab," he spoke as kicked through another batch of reeds. "And I suspect they could have easily gained entrance into your inn." He paused in his search and turned to look at her. "I have no time for games. Now tell me, have you seen the Israelites who are spying on our city?" She knew he was furious at the thought of them having been there, but a plan had suddenly formed in her mind, and she began to act on it.

"Israelites?" she questioned him, allowing a look of pure shock to cross her face.

"Are you certain the men you saw were Israelites?"

"Of course, I am certain," he stated loudly continuing to look right at her. "I have been pursuing them all day." His kicking had subsided, and just in time, he was mere inches from where Salmon lay hidden.

Rahab pretended to be astounded and walked slowly to the edge of the roof overlooking the city. Her plan to draw him away from the spies worked as Nazim began to stalk toward her and away from the men he had gotten so close to.

Through the darkness, she could make out Jenoah, standing at full attention, though he seemed almost awkward in his stance. She knew she had to get Nazim and all the soldiers away from her inn if she were going to free the spies. She closed her eyes in another quick and silent prayer before she spoke. When she did, it was as meek and as humbly as she knew how.

"They were Israelites?" she questioned in astonishment never taking her eyes from the street below and just loud enough for Nazim to hear.

"Were they here?" he asked, now standing by her side.

"They were," she admitted now looking up at him. Nazim took her by the shoulders, turning her to face him straight on. Looking into her eyes, he saw confusion and fear. She did not give him time to question her further but began speaking quickly. "They came late in the day, but I sent them away, Nazim, for I had never seen them before, and I have been so cautious since," she paused touching the back of her head. "They did not seek special favors," she continued, "but asked for lodging and food. I told them they could not stay here. I knew something was different about them," she shook her head as if she could hardly believe it, "but Israelites? Do you really think those men were the men you seek?"

Nazim looked deep into her eyes, and for an instant, she feared he would call her out in her lie. She must have looked more convincing than she felt.

"How long have they been gone?" he asked, turning as he spoke to descend the stairs back into the inn.

"They fled," she spoke quickly following after him. "It was close to nightfall, about the time of the shutting of the gate. I know not where they were going, but if you hurry, I have no doubt you can catch them," she spoke with urgency.

Nazim turned to her once again from his place at the bottom of the steps. He looked at her solemnly without a word, studying her features and looking deep into her eyes. Suddenly without another word, he turned, fleeing from the room. Her heart broke that she had lied to him, but what choice did she have? Perhaps after she got the spies out of the city and they returned to safety, she could talk to Nazim and make him understand as she had.

Rahab crossed her inn to the window and watched as Nazim ran into the street summoning

Jenoah to follow him. Few words were spoken before the two men began a steady jog toward the city gates. Rahab took a deep breath as the realization hit her. The time for the spies to escape had come.

Chapter Eleven

Rahab knew she had a little time before any of the soldiers would return to her inn. They would likely be gone for a few days in pursuit of the enemy they believed had gone out before them, but she wanted to act quickly. Racing back up the stairs to her rooftop, she paused long enough to do as she had witnessed Salmon do earlier. She quickly bowed her head and asked God to forgive her for lying to Nazim; an action, which she knew, would be frowned upon. She felt He was compassionate enough to do so; after all, she had done so to protect His men. Still, she was so unfamiliar with the ways of the Israelites and the God they served, and she did not wish to offend this God.

Once she reached the rooftop, she glanced over the edge to confirm neither Nazim nor any other officer had returned for some unknown reason. When she felt confident, she began the task of removing the reeds from the spies, quietly calling out to them as she did so. She had barely removed the first layer of the damp, smelly reeds from their bodies when both men bolted upright, inhaling the cool night air deeply.

"I thought you would never come!" Garrick finally announced once he felt he had enough air in his lungs to do so.

"I had to wait until I convinced Nazim you had been here and left. He believes he is following after you," she confessed, looking to Salmon. "It was the only way I could assure you could safely leave the city."

"We heard," Salmon admitted with a nod.

"Take heed," she continued, "Nazim will have everyone on high alert so we must get you out of here. Now!" She emphasized.

The men followed her back into the inn where she quickly gathered bread, cheese, and a few small containers of water into a basket. "You will need this," she clarified, handing them the basket of goods. "Go into the mountain and hide there for at least three days to assure you do not run into the soldiers who are pursuing you. Nazim will not rest until he has made every effort to find you. It will only be a few days before they return to Jericho, seeing as they took no food or rations with them. At that time, you should be able to safely return to your camp without fear of meeting them head on."

Garrick took the basket looking through the goods inside. Salmon could not take his eyes from the woman who had possibly given up everything to save them. He watched as she crossed the room and brought out a beautiful fabric, bound tightly and wound into a strong cord.

"Did you dye this," he asked in awe as he gently handled the beautiful material.

"I did," she smiled proudly. "It is the one piece I love too much to sell. I was saving it for a special occasion, though I honestly never planned to have an occasion for which I could use it." She handled the fabric delicately; while knowing with certainty it would be strong enough to handle the task for which it had been selected. "Tonight, this cord will lead you to safety, and I cannot imagine an occasion more worthy of its use," she admitted with surety. Rahab tied one end of the scarlet cord to a beam planted close to the window, letting the other end down the outside wall. "You must get to the mountain before the sun breaks the morning sky," she urged them. "Go quickly."

Garrick volunteered to go first, sensing there were words yet to be spoken between his leader and their rescuer. Slowly but efficiently he began his descent through the window and down the wall. Once assured he had reached the bottom, Salmon turned once more to Rahab with some final instructions.

"When we come again it will be to take this land, our Promised Land," he reminded her.

"Bind this line of scarlet once more in this window. This will be a sign to my men that you are to be kept safe. Have your father, mother, and siblings here, inside this house with you." Gently, he placed a hand on each of her shoulders to make sure he had her complete attention. "Rahab," he spoke plainly, looking straight into her eyes "anyone who goes into the street once our siege begins is not guaranteed sanctuary, but anyone who abides with you inside this house will be spared. I will come for you myself and lead you to safety. On this you have my word and my promise."

Rahab nodded in understanding. "The cord will remain in the window until you return. According to your words, so be it," she answered.

Salmon smiled a small smile. "I will see you again," he promised, and Rahab remembered hearing those same words from him at their first meeting.

"Go," she smiled in return. "And go carefully," she added. Salmon lifted his hand to touch her cheek and then moved to begin his descent down the wall. When he was safely on the ground, she pulled the cord up to lower the basket down to them. Her heart skipped a beat when Salmon touched his hand to his lips and then raised his hand to where she stood so far above in the window. It was a simple gesture of gratitude and appreciation, but his tenderness amazed her. She stood watching the pair as they descended into the darkness, almost wishing she had gone with them.

118

"Please keep them safe," she prayed aloud to the God she was learning to serve.

Suddenly realizing how tired she was, she turned from the window to ready herself for sleep, but when she closed her eyes, sleep would not come. She had so many questions. Not only about the God she was eager to learn more about, but also questions as to what her future now held. She had always had a plan, and though she was not proud of her profession, it had served her well financially. And were the day to ever come that she could not make her living by entertaining men, she had her flax field and her love of fabrics to sustain her.

Nazim had always been the face she saw when she thought of her future, the indirect but constant figure that she assumed would always be a part of her life. She knew deep down that he would never declare his affection for her publicly. For though she felt he did in fact harbor a love for her, she knew he loved his career and his stature with the king more. Yet if she could convince him that the God of the Israelites was the one true God, perhaps Nazim too could be saved along with her family when the Israelites came to take the city. They could survive together and begin a life on their own. Salmon had said anyone who was inside her house would be spared, did he not?

Salmon. The thought of him made her smile. With his gentle eyes and tender touch. Rahab turned onto her back with an audible sigh to stare at the ceiling. She was not naïve; she had caught him looking at her with interest on more than one occasion. But was that look one of admiration for her, or did his admiration stem simply from her ability to keep them safe and help them escape the city? He knew of her profession now, and she could tell he was very uncomfortable with it, yet he continued to look at her in a way that seemed he was looking past her imperfections and to the woman she was within. And there was no question that he was very handsome. She admitted to herself that he was every bit as handsome as Nazim.

Nazim leaped into her mind again. "Enough," she said aloud to herself as the men unknowingly battled for control of her mind. Frustrated with her thoughts, she moved from her cot to the window where the scarlet cord still hung. Would Nazim ever forgive her were he to discover her lies to him regarding the spies? Looking into the darkness, she decided she needed a plan: something to divert her restless mind from the men who continually wrestled for occupancy there. Once the spies returned to their camp, she was not sure how much time she would have before they would arrive to capture the city, but her family had to be with her inside her house before that time came. She knew with certainty that she had at least three days. Tomorrow she would go to her father's house and speak to her family in an effort to convince them of all she now believed and urge them to come into her home.

With a plan in place and hope in her heart, she stretched out once again on her cot, yet sleep continued to elude her. Could she ever convince her family to believe her? And once Nazim returned was there even a possibility she would be able to convince him as well? Mental exhaustion finally won out. Pulling the covers over her body, she fell into a night of restless sleep and troubled dreams.

The next morning dawned bright and clear. Rahab was up before the sun, unable to gain more than an hour or two of sleep. Her heart raced as troubling thoughts began to crowd her mind the deeper she lay into the night. Finally, she had given up and rose to tidy her rooms and prepare for the trip to her father's.

She gathered a few small items and the little coin she had accumulated since her last visit then made her way through the city streets. She had grown accustomed to seeing the soldiers on their normal patrol, but things were very different today. The only visible soldiers were those of a lesser rank. Nazim, Jenoah, and the others of their caliber continued their search for the spies outside the city gates. Rahab recognized that things could easily become even less civil than normal were others to realize that their city was under less protection.

She moved quickly, pulling her drab-colored veil around her face. She did not want to give anyone cause to notice her, so she did not linger on her journey. She had left early enough that the streets were not as crowded as before, and she made a mental note that this time of day was a much better time of day to reach her destination quickly.

She prayed as she journeyed for words of wisdom, that her family would listen to her with an open mind and understanding, and most of all for them to be accepting of the God of the Israelites. Her father's temper was often very quick, and she was not sure how he would handle her confession of forsaking the gods he had taught her to serve, or of her declaration that the Israelites would overcome their city. It did not take long for her to reach her father's house, and she saw him headed to the stables as she approached.

"Rahab?" he questioned happily, pausing when he noticed her. "We did not expect you today. Your mother will be excited to see you!" he exclaimed as he greeted his daughter in a warm embrace. Rahab returned his embrace holding her father a little tighter than normal.

"Is something wrong?" he asked, sensing such and pulling away from her.

"I need to speak with you and mother," she admitted, "together. Do you have a few minutes you could spare for me?" she asked humbly.

"Of course, daughter," he agreed without hesitation as he led her into their home. "Your brothers and sister have gone on errands this morning so you could not have arrived at a better time."

"Rahab!" her mother exclaimed at their entry. "What brings you back so soon?" she asked, excited to see her daughter once again. At the looks on the faces of her daughter and husband, she paused in her task of kneading dough. Brushing her hands on a nearby cloth, she approached them quickly. "What is it?" she asked, fear creeping into her voice as her husband motioned for her to take the seat beside him.

Rahab cleared her throat, offered up yet another silent prayer, and began. She paused for a moment as she realized the calmness that had come over her heart had been poured out by the God she had chosen to serve, the God she had come to tell her family of. How wonderful to serve such a God. With a small smile, she began.

"I need to speak to the two of you regarding a very important matter." Rahab saw her mother begin to blink rapidly, a sure sign she was uncomfortable and knew she believed Rahab was about to confess a deep secret to her parents. However, she had already made her confessions to her Heavenly Father regarding her profession and had no plans to share those same secrets with her parents today. She laid a hand over her mothers. "It is no secret I have done well selling my fabrics and materials, and I am happy to have been able to supplement your income, Father, with my own. However, the amount I am able to provide to you will no doubt begin to lessen over the next few weeks. I have decided to, cut back," she finally decided on the words, "on the amount of work I do."

"This is what concerns you, Rahab?" her father asked sincerely. "That you will not be able to bring as much in the way of finances to our family?" He waved her worries aside, her mother sighing in audible relief.

"Do not worry yourself about that, daughter," she smiled. "We will be fine!" she assured her as she moved to rise.

"That is not the only reason I have come," Rahab interrupted, pulling her mother back into the chair from where she had risen. She decided to jump right into the heart of the conversation. "Father, do you remember the last time I was here and the conversation we had about the Israelites who had made camp on the other side of the Jordan?"

"I do," he confirmed, settling back in his chair, curious as to where his daughter was heading with such a topic.

"I have come to speak with you concerning those rumors," Rahab admitted. "I am convinced the stories we have heard are completely true, and the rumors we have heard are actually facts." Rahab took in the confused look on both of her parents' faces. She was going to have to be straightforward and spoke slowly. "I have met, and talked at length, to one of the Israelites. He has told me of their journey across the desert, of the victories they have won, and of their plans to take our city, but most importantly he has told me of the God they serve. Their God is forgiving and protective over His people; He is wise and loving and just—completely unlike the idols we have been taught to serve." She feared the impact her next statement may have on her parents, but it was, after all, the reason she had come. "I have decided that I will serve their God as well," she finished plainly.

"Rahab!" her mother exclaimed. "You would so easily forsake the gods of Jericho simply because someone you barely know has frightened you with threats against our people? You know how protected our city is!"

"Mother I had forsaken the gods you had taught me of many years ago," she admitted plainly.

Her father was remaining surprisingly calm. "Your reasons for doing so?" he asked simply.

"I have never understood the sacrifices and rituals that were expected of our gods in the temple," she admitted. "They are simple idols and statues created by our ancestors. I always felt empty when I left there. Like everything sacrificed was in vain. Why did we continue to sacrifice to a statue we could move about, or even destroy, if we so chose to. My life seemed full, yet I felt completely void. I have known for a long time that something was missing. I have not practiced those sacrifices and rituals for many years. None at all actually since I left you and mother to begin my life with Nariman," she directed to her Father whom she was afraid was about to end the conversation. She decided to change the subject for a moment and work her faith into it again at a later time. "And though I sincerely hope you will at least consider my beliefs, this is also not the only reason I have come. I came to ask you to come into my home."

Her mother shook her head in confusion and Rahab knew she was throwing a lot at them in a very short period of time; yet, she had no idea how much time she would actually have. Her father spoke no words but looked at her as if she had taken leave of her senses. Rahab rose to cross the room and then turned back to look at her parents directly.

"The Israelites will take our city," she said pointedly. "Our land has been promised to them by the God they serve. The same God who led them through the Red Sea on dry land, the same God who helped them to defeat the Amorites, is the very same God who will lead them to destroy Jericho and obtain this land He has promised them. Salmon has promised me, because I have protected him, that all who dwell inside my house will remain safe. Everyone else within the city walls shall perish."

"How did you protect this Israelite?" her father finally asked.

"He and another of his men had come inside the gates to spy on our fortresses and soldiers. I hid them on my roof until they could escape to safety. I told Nazim they had left before

126

him when he came searching my inn for them," she explained.

"And how does your new God feel about your lying to the king's Chief Centurion?" her father questioned.

"As I said, He is a forgiving God," Rahab spoke with confidence, "and I only did what was necessary to protect His men. Nazim would have had no mercy on them had they been found."

Surprisingly, her father seemed to be contemplating all she had told them instead of losing his temper as she had expected.

"Rahab," her mother broke the silence, "I thought at our last conversation that you perhaps had some sort of feelings for this...Nazim. Will you warn him as you have your father and me?" she asked. "Why not warn everyone in the city?" she asked finally.

"I have not yet decided how I will handle Nazim," she admitted. "He is still beyond the gates searching for the Israelite spies. I do plan to tell him of my decision to follow the God of the Israelites, but it will depend upon how he handles that information as to whether or not I tell him of the impending doom upon Jericho. I will not give up the Israelites or their plan to take our city. And no matter if I shout the warning I have been given from the rooftop, you both know as well as I do that no one in the city would pay me any heed," she finished with certainty.

"And you truly believe this band of wandering slaves will be able to breach our impassable walls and conquer our land?" This

127

question came from her father, who looked squarely into her eyes as he spoke.

Rahab did not flinch as she answered. "With my entire being."

"And how do you expect He will be able to complete this task?" he asked.

"I do not know," she spoke honestly. "But I know that He will," she continued. "How did He dry up the Red Sea? How did He lead the Israelites in victory over the Amorites? How did He send me here at just the exact moment you and mother would be open to this conversation, and how is it that you know in your heart that all I say is true and that you are actually considering coming with me?" she asked plainly.

Rahab's heart pounded in her chest as the silence between them hung like a weight in the air. Her father rose and crossed to the window overlooking the land he owned. Finally, he turned to look at her mother who sat watching him, a solitary tear rolling along her cheek.

"We have heard all our daughter has to say," he began.

"Shall we go?" her mother asked, interrupting him and looking to the man who had led her with love for so many years. Their way had not always been easy, and they had made many mistakes in their lifetime together, but he had always done what he thought was best for them at the moment, even when he was wrong.

"I do not understand why I feel as I do," he admitted. "But I feel we should heed the warning." He turned his attention from his wife to his daughter. "We shall make our preparations and join you before the week's end."

Chapter Twelve

Two days had passed since Rahab had visited her family and convinced them to come live in her home. The night she had returned, a regular guest had arrived requesting her services, which she had easily turned away. To turn Nazim away, however, would take a lot more strength, and a part of her hoped her parents would already be residing in her home before that moment came. It would make things a lot easier.

Her father had promised her they would arrive before the end of the week, but she expected Nazim to return at any time now and had a strong feeling his arrival would come before that of her parents. She had no indication as to how correct her intuition would be.

Rahab had just finished heating broth for her dinner when she heard the familiar knock at the back door of her inn. Nazim was back, and he was here. Turning slowly, she gazed into the looking glass he had given her as she passed by it smoothing her hair. The reflection reminded her that she was a different person than when she had last seen him. She was now a follower of Jehovah God and no longer the harlot, or even the same woman, who he was accustomed to visiting. She straightened the pendent always present around her neck and proceeded to the door.

With a quick prayer, she opened the portal with a smile, which quickly faded as she noticed immediately how worn Nazim looked. His hair was a mess, all over his head, instead of being pulled tightly back in a leather strap as usual. His eyes were weary and tired, and his cheeks sunken. Her heart broke for him at his appearance, but she also felt a sense of relief. The man before her was in no way rejoicing over the capture of the Israeli spies. At that thought, she felt a small smile return to her lips. The spies were safe.

"You look horrible," she spoke honestly as she moved to allow him entrance. Nazim stepped into the room but said nothing. He took the offered chair she motioned toward and sat with his elbows on the table, placing his head in his hands. Without asking, she poured him a large bowl of steaming broth and set it before him, also cutting a slice from the bread her mother had given her during her visit.

"Eat," she commanded softly. "You cannot rest or think clearly on an empty stomach."

Nazim glanced at her and released the invisible breath he had been holding. He stirred the broth she had set before him, encouraging it to cool, as she took the seat directly across from him. Allowing him time with his thoughts she thought through her next words carefully. Over the years she had known him she had seen him tired before. He was the king's chief centurion; battles were not something he ran from. A few he had lost temporarily, though that was not the normal fate, but most he had rather easily won. She had seen him concerned over political affairs, and she had seen him angry more times than she could count, yet she had never seen him like this. He was worn beyond tired, exhausted even, but more than that, he was discouraged. Though it assured Rahab the spies were safe, seeing Nazim like this did not bring her joy. It broke her heart in a very real way. He spoke before she could decide on the right words to say.

"We lost them," he finally admitted softly, continuing to slowly stir the broth before him. "We tracked them all the way to the fords of the Jordan River and did not find so much as a trace of them. It is as if they disappeared before us." Rahab sat quietly letting him speak. He said the words as he stared into the broth before him as if he himself could not believe them. "I just cannot understand how we could not even find so much as a footprint," he continued. "Jenoah is the best tracker among us, and even he could not spot a single trace of them." He sighed deeply, shook his head, and began to sip the broth slowly.

"What will you do now?" Rahab asked, after a moment.

Nazim shook his head. "I have instructed my men to return to their homes and meet me at the palace in the morning. Jenoah and I will brief the king and make decisions at that time. He will not be pleased." He finished his meal in silence and then sat back in his chair, the bowl before him empty. He stretched his long legs out before him and placed his hands at the back of his head.

"Thank you for the meal," he smiled to her finally, and Rahab marveled at the gentleness the smile brought to his face in spite of his massive size. "You have been back to your parent's?" he asked, realizing for the first time the fresh bread he had just finished.

"I have," she spoke simply, hoping he would not press the issue further by asking too many questions.

"Are they well," he asked a quizzical look crossing his features.

"They are," she answered simply again.

Nazim shook his head in affirmation, letting the matter drop, then rose and crossed the room to look out the window facing the street. It was late enough that he was not worried about being spotted from below, as the streets were empty. He stood for a moment lost in thought, and Rahab wondered where the evening was headed. *"Jehovah, please help me remain strong.*

Help me to remain faithful to you though what I really want is to bring Nazim joy. Please give me the right words to say and the strength to reject him if the time comes," she prayed silently.

As if he could read her thoughts, Nazim turned to her and crossed the room to where she remained seated, her back to him. He moved her hair from where it hung loose and began to massage her shoulders. She felt him lean and whisper into her ear.

"I have missed you," he spoke quietly. "Join me for a bath," he prompted as he kissed her ear.

She closed her eyes for only an instant when she remembered the prayer she had just prayed. Gently pulling away from him, she answered honestly. "I have missed you as well, but we need to talk," she admitted as she patted his hand where it rested on her shoulder and stood. His touch seriously weakened her defenses, and she knew she must keep distance between them. He misunderstood her movement and pulled her close into a tender yet passionate kiss. Again, she pulled away, though it took every fiber of her being, confusing him as he moved to lift her.

"Nazim, wait," she commanded him gently. "We need to talk," she pleaded with him.

"Then we will talk as we bathe," he answered, pulling off his vest revealing his bare chest and torso and approaching her once again. Rahab pressed her hands against his toned abdomen.

"We will talk," she answered clearly, "fully clothed and in this room." She retrieved his vest from the chair he had tossed it onto and handed it back to him where he stood dumbstruck in front of her.

"Rahab," he began with a deep sigh as he reluctantly pulled his vest back over his head. "Is it necessary that you choose this moment to be cantankerous?" The look that crossed her face said more than any words could have. "I am sorry," he apologized quickly knowing that look. "I am just tired, and I want nothing more at this moment than to clear my mind and ease my tension by enjoying a nice bath and some time with you."

The physical side of Rahab ached to bring him happiness, to bathe with him, to pleasure him, and then to spend the night wrapped in his arms safe and secure. But the spiritual side of her knew that to engage in any kind of physical activity with this man, or any man outside of wedlock was wrong and would go against the God she had chosen to serve.

"Nazim," she began as she moved to put some distance between them once again. "I need to talk with you about something, and it cannot wait," she began earnestly. "I am a different person than I was before you left to track the spies."

"Is something wrong?" he asked, alarm filling his voice. "Are you ill?" He crossed to where she stood, his physical desire for her being replaced by very real concern. He placed his

136

hands on her arms and turned her toward him, searching her face for answers. "Are you with child?" he asked suddenly.

The concern for her well-being that had clearly replaced his physical longing melted her heart, yet when he moved to pull her close, she gently pushed away from him once more.

"No, I am not with child, and there is nothing wrong with me physically," she assured him. Then, for a moment, she paused, allowing her mind to linger on his last question. The thought that she could become pregnant had never occurred to her. Had God protected her in yet another way even before she chose to follow Him? How would she have ever survived with a child? Had her carnal sins left her barren? The questions swirled in her mind, almost causing her to forget the discussion she was in the middle of. Quickly she brought her mind back to the present.

"Nazim, I have made a decision. I will no longer entertain guests. I will make my way dying and selling my fabrics, but I will not be exchanging physical pleasantries for money any longer," she spoke plainly and with surety.

He stood before her clearly trying to process what she was telling him. "But I am not a regular 'guest,'" he spoke emphasizing the word. "You will allow me to be your 'exclusive guest?'" he smiled as he questioned.

Rahab could not help but chuckle at the way his features had turned this giant man into a young boy.

"No, Nazim," she began, "you are not a regular guest. It is no secret to either of us that you have been and continue to be so much more to me. But I can no longer entertain you, or any man, in that way. It is not right, and I will no longer go against Jehovah God in that fashion."

She watched as the words she had just spoken resonated in his mind and watched as anger began to replace the concern he had shown for her. She was not clear if he was upset over her rejection or the fact that she had recognized Jehovah as her God. He closed his eyes and turned away from her crossing to the window nearest him that faced the Jordan.

The minutes he stared across the horizon in silence seemed like hours before he finally turned to her. His mind had been wondering, pondering over all she had said. Yet it was the mention of Jehovah God that had sparked his anger. She did not miss the fact that his hand had gone instinctively to the hilt of his sword.

"Jehovah God," he stated calmly, though she recognized it for the question that was coming. "The God of the Israelites?"

"Yes," she spoke with confidence. She lowered her eyes for a moment before gathering the strength to look at him again.

"Tell me, Rahab," he said as he slowly began advancing toward her. "How is it that you have come to serve this, Jehovah God?" he asked slowly. His voice was as thick as steel, and for the first time since she had known him, she felt fear at his approach. "Who has taught you enough about this God that you have chosen to abandon the gods of Jericho and to serve Him so completely?"

Rahab stood tall as he approached, straightening her shoulders and keeping her eyes locked with his at all times. "Nazim, listen to me," she began, never letting down her defenses. "There are so many things that point to Him as the one true God and if you would allow me to share with you all the things Salmon has shared with me..."

"Salmon!" he interrupted so boldly that she jumped. He was now directly in front of her looking down into her face. "This, Salmon, he is one of the Israelite spies, I presume?" he asked, and she saw the menacing look in his eyes. "One of the 'men' who stopped by, the men who you sent away so quickly?" he accused.

"He is," she answered truthfully, and her voice was clear though her heart was about to beat from her chest.

"And when have you had such a conversation with 'Salmon,'" he mocked, "that he had time to convince you so easily to become a traitor to the gods of our nation?"

For a brief moment, she wondered if she could soften Nazim's thoughts toward those he considered their enemies were she to tell him how Salmon had been her rescuer outside the gates not so many days ago. Seeing the menacing look on his face, she feared it would be useless, but still, she had to try. If Nazim cared for her as he claimed he did, perhaps...

"I had a conversation with one of the Israelites, his name is Salmon," she clarified, "on the way home from my parent's house when I visited them the time before this last time," she spoke honestly.

Nazim thought back, his brows knit in confusion. He remembered finding her bleeding after that visit. "It was an Israelite who attacked you!" he accused through clenched teeth, his eyes suddenly fierce.

"No!" she quickly defended, "an Israelite is who rescued me! If it were not for him, Nazim, I would more than likely be dead by now. Thanks be to Jehovah God that Salmon arrived when he did!"

Nazim looked as if he had been slapped. It broke her heart that she was causing him to feel betrayal, but she had to make him see.

"Nazim, things are not as we have always believed," she continued trying desperately to convince him. "Look at the condition our city is in under the rule of the gods we have been taught to serve. There is no peace and spirituality here. Our people sacrifice to pieces of stone! Without you in the streets, there is nothing but chaos, thievery, and assault. Nazim, I believe the things Salmon has told me of the God they serve. He is loving and forgiving, and He is as powerful as He is protective." Rahab placed her hands on Nazim's forearms; her eyes pleading with him to listen to her. "Perhaps this land HAS been promised to the Israelites, and if we would surrender it peacefully, they could tell us more of their God and…"

Nazim jerked away from her so quickly that she jumped. "Have you lost your mind, Rahab?" he asked, beginning to raise his voice. "Do you even hear the senseless words you utter?"

Rahab stood looking at him as humbly as she knew how.

"I do, Nazim. If you would just talk to them, just listen to them. They are kind and good and…"

"I cannot believe the nonsense I am hearing from you!" He interrupted her with a shout, turning from her again while working to keep his anger in check. Quickly he crossed to the second window overlooking the Jordan River. It was at that moment he noticed the scarlet cord. Pausing suddenly at his discovery, he reached out and toyed with the cord from where it hung, a thought struck him so suddenly that it sickened him. She could not have. She would not have. Turning slowly, he stared at her for a moment before he spoke somewhat calmer, almost too calm, as the stark realization of it all hit him. He was not an ignorant man.

"Rahab," he asked as he held the cord, pain evident in his voice, "What have you done? How could you help them escape?" Rahab felt the tears that filled her eyes. "And how could you speak such indulgent words of their God?" he continued. There had to be a reason she felt as strongly as she did. Some way they had gained such power over her. Was it sorcery? Trickery?

"What have they done to you?" he asked, crossing to her once again this time reaching out to grab her shoulders. His eyes blazed with anger. He did not hurt her, but his grip was firm.

"They have done nothing to me, Nazim, except tell me of their God," she promised looking up at him. "Did you not hear me say Salmon rescued me?"

"And how many times have I rescued you?" he argued, his voice now thundering. "Yet one of them shows up once, when you have yet again placed yourself in a dangerous situation, and you are ready to surrender our land to them? This land that I have spent my life protecting!" He continued in his rage before she could speak, his anger now fully heightened. "We have searched for these intruders for days! They are a serious threat to our people and to our city, and you helped them escape! All because you have a new 'revelation' that the God they serve is the one true God because 'Salmon' told you so."

"Nazim, listen to me," she pleaded.

"What do you expect of me Rahab?" he interrupted before she could begin, "do you expect me to run to the King proclaiming we should just hand our land over to them and serve their God because one of them has 'rescued' the city whore!"

Finally, he completely lost the control he had been fighting for as he pulled back and recklessly released his fist into the wall behind her. Rahab jumped as wood splintered around her.

Never before had he had such a violent outburst of anger. Never before had he spoken to her in such a tone and referred to her in such a way. Nothing he had said was untrue; yet coming from him it cut her to the core. She stared straight at him, standing tall, her eyes never leaving his, yet she could not stop the tears, which escaped and rolled freely along her face. He saw those tears and the pain in her eyes, and he knew nothing he could say would ever make up for the way he had spoken to her or the act of violence he had portrayed.

He turned from her, not being able to bear looking at her this moment. He was as hurt by her betrayal as she was at the words he had spoken. Turning brought him in full view of the cord still hanging in the window. He could not stay here. He had to get out. Quickly, he stalked past her without looking at her face again, but paused when he gained the door.

"I will be leaving town tomorrow as soon as I brief the king," he spoke with surety over his shoulder. "I do not know when I will return."

She did not turn around to look at him as he spoke. She did not turn around as he opened the portal. She did not turn around as she heard the door close firmly behind him. She did not turn around as she heard his footsteps descend the stairs.

How she did not know, but she knew with certainty, she would never get the chance to speak to Nazim again. Her world crumbled around her at the realization. She had lost him, and in doing so, she had lost the chance to ever win him to the God she had chosen. She collapsed to the floor in a heap and sobbed aloud to her God.

Chapter Thirteen

Salmon and Garrick sat with Joshua, Caleb, and other prominent men of their camp around a campfire a little less than one week after their departure to spy on Jericho. Once again, Salmon had used the earth as his canvas, drawing out the fortress of the city before them. His speculations had been confirmed. The city was well fortified, and he relayed that message to the men before him.

"It will not be an easy city to take," he spoke plainly. "Once we breach those walls, the centurions within are powerful men. Yet," he grinned, "our reputation precedes us."

"In what way?" Joshua asked.

"They fear us," he confirmed, "but more than us, they fear our God. We were told that the men of the city 'tremble in fear at the stories they have heard and at the miracles performed by our

God,' " he quoted Rahab. "I feel that will give us the vantage point needed to overcome them. But," he reemphasized, "it will not be an easy task."

"Our God never takes the easy way out," Joshua reminded them once again, dismissing the problem. "He will make a way. But" he continued with complete honesty, "I must pray and seek Jehovah's guidance on how we will proceed. Until then, we must continue to build the spirits of our people and encourage them. They grow restless once more."

"The people are tired," Caleb confirmed. "We have wandered for so long,"

"Indeed," Joshua nodded, "yet the time grows near! I feel God will show us the way very soon," he spoke with certainty. Joshua's positive attitude was infectious. It was his demeanor alone on days that the wanderers felt so far from God that kept their hope alive that one day they would finally reach their Promised Land. Without Joshua, they would all have returned to Egypt and to the bondage of slavery they had escaped. Salmon prayed that he could become half the man Joshua was.

"There is one person within the city that we must save at all cost," Salmon began. He took the next half hour to tell the men how Rahab had kept them safe. He explained the way she had hid them on her roof, sent the centurion called Nazim away, and helped them escape the city under cover of night. "And, Joshua," Salmon concluded, "she has forsaken the gods of her people, believing that our God is the one true God. I believe her conversion is real, and I assured her that we will keep her, as well as all inside her home, safe throughout the battle."

"Then we shall," Joshua promised him. "How will we know her home from the others? You said there are multiple homes inside the walls."

"She is a…seamstress," Salmon acknowledged preferring that be the only of her occupations he share openly. Garrick nodded respecting his ally and friend for his discretion.

"A scarlet cord hangs visibly from her window," Salmon continued. "I instructed her to leave it there so we can easily distinguish her home from the others."

"We will spread the word," Joshua spoke, signaling to the other men around the fire. "Those who reside behind the window where the scarlet cord is hung shall be kept safe from harm."

"And what will become of this young lady once the battle is over?" Caleb questioned Salmon with a smile.

"I suppose time will tell the ending of the story," Salmon chuckled to the older man whom he so admired.

Garrick placed a hand playfully on Salmon's shoulder. "Before I met her myself, I had heard of the 'maid with raven black hair and eyes as deep as the sea,'" he playfully mocked recalling Salmon's words from before. The whole group laughed aloud at the shade of red that could be seen covering Salmon's face, even by the glow of the fire. "I must admit," Garrick continued, "that Salmon did not stretch the truth. I daresay her countenance is as beautiful as her face."

As the group dispersed a few moments later, Salmon found himself alone with Joshua. He felt he should confide in the leader he so adored.

"Joshua, I feel it is only right to be completely honest with you and let you know that Rahab previously engaged in acts of prostitution as well as her occupation of being a seamstress," he explained. "Yet, as I stated before, I honestly feel her conversion is real and that she will no longer practice such acts."

Joshua looked to the young man he had watched grow during their time in the wilderness and marveled at his maturity.

"I would expect as much in as wicked of a city as Jericho has become. Salmon, if God Himself has chosen to forgive her, who am I to stand in the way. If He can part the waters of the Red Sea, lead His wandering children through the desert for forty years using a cloud by day and a pillar of fire by night, all the while feeding us with manna from Heaven, who am I to say He cannot redeem a harlot and do a mighty work within her." He slapped the younger man on the back. "If you seek God's favor in this union and choose to wed her once we are safe within the Promised Land, I will gladly give you my blessing. Do not rush into a marriage, however, simply because you feel sorry for her and for the life she has endured. God has a plan for this woman, as He has already shown by using her to keep you and Garrick safe. All I ask is that you seek and consider His will in this and in every aspect of your life," he concluded.

"Yes, sir," Salmon confirmed, "I would have it no other way."

The men parted then, Joshua into his tent to pray and seek God's direction and Salmon to his own to do the same.

The king sat on his throne toying with his scepter. "I am not pleased, Nazim," he spoke harshly. "I expected more—of you especially. I expected the heads before me of the men who dared breach my city walls, and instead, I get cowering soldiers making apologies for their weakness!"

Nazim stood before the throne; Jenoah at his side. He expected the king's temperament to be exactly as it was.

"Your Majesty, I feel our best method of attack cannot be decided upon until we disclose all information possible about our enemy," he spoke with certainty attempting to redirect the king's focus.

"We have heard plenty of information about these people and the miraculous God they serve," he thundered. "What more is there to know?"

"The Israelites must have a weakness, Majesty, regardless of their God. If you would allow me, I would like to travel to the land of the Amorites. I will discover for myself exactly how they were defeated, study the strategies used by the Israelites, talk with surviving Amorites, and find what weakness they possess. Then I shall return here knowing better how to destroy them and how to protect our land."

"Leave our city?" the king asked in utter amazement at such a request. "You wish to leave our city when on our borders are enemies who have conquered every city they have gone to battle with? And who do you suggest will protect our city when they decide to conquer us and you are on your 'journey of discovery?'" he mocked.

The king was on his feet pacing before his throne. Nazim was quite certain were his scepter replaced with a sword both he and Jenoah would have already lost their heads.

"Your Majesty, it is never my intention to leave our city unprotected," Nazim encouraged him. "Jenoah is quite capable of handling things in my absence, and I would only be gone for a few weeks. I do not feel our enemies will advance during that time, for the Jordan, which separates their camp from our city, is at flood stage. The water is far too deep for their band of soldiers to attempt a crossing. Besides, the spies must know we were tracking them and that they barely escaped us," he lied. "I do not feel they would be so bold as to approach again so soon."

The king laughed maliciously. "What I feel, Nazim," he spat as he approached his chief centurion, "is that you are afraid." Nazim could not believe the gumption of the small man who had placed himself in a position in which he had to look up at one of his people. Only when their king had lost his temper would he fail to remain in a position above them at all times. Instead, in his immature haste, he approached the men before him.

Nazim dared not look down at his king, though he towered over him, for that would inadvertently call him out. Instead, he looked straight ahead; realizing the only defense the king had was his political stature. He was protected by nothing more than a small ring of metal upon his head, a crown that Nazim fantasized about capturing and easily manipulating into a noose he would wind around the cowering man's neck, but the tiny man was his king and Nazim would not forget his place.

"Are you afraid, Nazim?" the king scoffed at him, emphasizing his words.

"The only fear I have, Your Majesty," Nazim spoke calmly as he stared straight ahead, "is of disappointing you and the people of our city."

"Then face your fear!" the king screamed, emphasizing each word. "For you have disappointed me!" Nazim did not move, but the king did not miss the clenching of his jaw.

Slowly he began to back away from the man in front of him realizing, though he would

151

never admit it, that he may be pushing his best soldier a bit too far. After all, he recognized that this man could harm him easily if he chose to. He approached his throne and took his place, straightening his crown. After a moment, he broke the silence.

"Go, if you feel you must," he spoke abruptly dismissing them both with a wave of his hand. He was tired of yelling for the moment. "Find a survivor from the most recent victims of the Israelis and discover their weakness. But do not," he commanded, "return into my presence unless you can assure me a victory, or your head will be the one on a platter before me," he promised.

Nazim bowed his head and turned from the king without a word, Jenoah doing the same and following him quickly. Neither of the men spoke a word until they were outside the palace gates. Once they were in the streets of Jericho, Jenoah called out to his leader and friend. Nazim stopped abruptly turning to face him.

"Are you certain you should be leaving town now?" Jenoah asked plainly. "I understand the convincing way you spoke to the king, but the Israelites have shown no fear as of yet, and I have no reason to believe they will begin to now. If their spies made it across the river, their soldiers could," he spoke quietly but fervently.

"Then I must go quickly," Nazim answered solidly as he scanned the street and turned to walk toward his quarters. He did not pause as he gained his home but walked straight through the door, Jenoah following behind him. He grabbed a small sack and began to fill it with provisions for his journey.

"Nazim, what exactly are you expecting to find?" Jenoah asked, watching curiously as his captain tossed more than one knife into the sack.

"Answers," he spoke bluntly never pausing in his task. Throwing the sack across his back and tucking yet another knife into his belt strap by his sword, he turned and looked at the only man he considered a friend.

"Watch carefully for changes in the enemy camp while I am gone," he instructed. "And keep an especially attentive eye on Rahab's inn," he commanded.

"Rahab?" Jenoah questioned as Nazim exited the door. He ran to catch up to him. Stopping him with a hand to his elbow, Jenoah questioned his leader again as he was about to mount his horse. "Rahab, the harlot?"

Nazim stood where Jenoah had stopped him and looked toward the home of the woman he loved but no longer knew. He knew that now was not the time to sort through his feelings of betrayal, perhaps there would be time for that as he traveled. But he knew that he loved her, and he knew that they had hurt one another in ways he was not sure they could ever get past. The time was not right for him to go to her and attempt to make amends, for what he had said, nor was he ready to. He also knew now was not the time to divulge his secret to his friend.

He spoke plainly as he climbed onto the back of his steed. "I have reason to believe she knows more than she has told us," he finished as he urged his horse forward. Jenoah watched as he went, but something told him that answers regarding defeating their enemies were not the only answers Nazim was seeking; he was seeking answers to his own personal dilemmas as well.

Looking to the window of the harlot in the inn above him, his speculation was confirmed. Jenoah watched as she approached the window, arms locked in front of her, looking down at the street below. She watched his captain carefully as he moved through the street, approached the gates, and then left the city. Even at this distance, Jenoah noticed the sadness that marked her features, and he did not miss when she reached to wipe the tears from her beautiful face.

Chapter Fourteen

Nazim was gone, and regardless of how she replayed the scene with him in her mind, she was not sure how she could have made anything any better. Rahab struggled with the possibility of never seeing him again, and though her heart ached at the thought, she had completely surrendered her life to God and trusted Him with her future. Salmon had told her she could pray about anything at any time. She could pray for Nazim, and she would, every day of her life.

To take her mind from her pain, she threw herself into readying her home for her family. She went through her belongings and parted with anything that marked her former life as a harlot. When possible, she made adjustments to garments that she liked, so that she could continue to use them on a daily basis. She enjoyed her time sewing and mending, bringing new life to items she that had once kept hidden for times in the darkness. It was therapy for her weary mind.

Two days after Nazim had left, her parents, her brothers, and her sister arrived. She greeted them warmly, but with grave anticipation of the things to come. They discussed what little she knew of the God she had chosen, and in coming into her home, they had proven their minds were open to what she had to say and what she now believed.

"How long will we have before the Israelites advance upon the city?" her father questioned after dinner.

"I do not know," Rahab answered honestly. "Salmon gave no indication as to a time of the attack, and truthfully, I am not even sure that he knows. A man called Joshua leads them. All I know is that he encouraged me to get you here as soon as possible to ensure your safety." Her siblings had retired to a back room where they would sleep, allowing the conversation with her parents to be open and honest.

"And Nazim?" her mother asked, delicately approaching the subject. Rahab closed her eyes at the mention of his name.

"My conversation with Nazim did not go well," she finally admitted. She had covered the damage he had caused to the wall, not wishing to elaborate on the subject with her family. "He has left the city; I expect in search of information on the Israeli people. I have no indication as to when, or if, he will return." She lowered her eyes, hoping to disguise the tears pooling there.

"I am so sorry, Rahab," her mother spoke sincerely reaching to take her daughter's hand. "I could tell you thought very highly of him."

Rahab blinked away her tears and attempted a small smile. She then moved from the table to the stairs in order to change the subject.

"Come, Father," she spoke, turning her attention to him. "Come see the flax drying on my rooftop. The harvest was good this year, and I will be able to use your help in turning the reeds into fabric," she continued as she led him up the stairs to the roof.

From here her father could clearly see the fires of the Israeli camp, which was her full intention for bringing him up.

"They are just on the other side of the Jordan, as we have heard," he spoke quietly to himself in amazement. He had believed the reports he had been given, and the news that had come straight from his daughter, but to see it with his own eyes was surreal.

"I do not expect we have much time, Father," she confirmed as she watched the fires glow in the distance. She wondered which fire Salmon sat around this night.

"The waters of the Jordan are high," he noticed aloud, looking for anything that would possibly delay an attack. "The banks are overflowing with the spring floods. I cannot imagine they will cross until the water has begun to subside," he speculated, looking to his daughter for her reaction.

"I do not expect the waters of the Jordan to be much of a problem for a God who parted the Red Sea," she reminded him gently. She pulled her shawl closer to her body, the cool night air causing a shiver to run along her frame. Though she would not admit it, there was something inside her giving her the assurance that something was about to happen, regardless as to the depth of the waters that lay before them.

She and her father spoke well into the night of possible scenarios and battle plans, neither of them having an inkling of what to expect. And though they were both relying on Salmon's word to keep them safe, each of them was equally fearful of the unknown.

The next morning, Rahab and her father returned to the rooftop. They had discussed the matter, and both felt it would be best to continue with their daily business until the arrival of the Israelites was imminent. Today they would begin the task of beating the dried flax causing the reeds to separate into fine fibers from which they would make fabric. Her mother, brothers, and sister would aid them in the arduous task.

As she was accustomed to doing each time, she reached the rooftop, Rahab looked toward the Israeli camp for any signs of activity there. What she saw both excited and alarmed

158

her. There was movement, a lot of movement, as the entire body of wandering Israelites moved forward closing in on the banks of the Jordan River. Men on horseback went before them, she assumed shouting orders, though the distance was far too great for her to hear. Before them came a company of men bearing a large gold chest, carried on golden rods. *That must be the Ark of the Covenant Salmon had mentioned*, she thought to herself. Surrounding the chest were men in robes bearing what looked, from this distance, to be rams horn trumpets.

Rahab shielded her eyes from the sun and strained to make out the details. The sun glistened off the golden chest catching the eye of anyone who was within view. Her family had joined her, and as she looked around, she noticed much of the city had taken to their rooftops as well, watching in anticipation as to what was happening on the banks of the Jordan River.

As they watched, the men carrying the Ark of the Covenant continued their trek into the water.

"They will drown themselves," one of her brothers exclaimed. "The river is well above flood stage!"

"Quiet," her Father commanded as though he too felt something miraculous was about to happen. "Watch and see," he commanded softly, never taking his eyes from the scene which was playing out before them.

The party continued their advance into the river, the water rushing before them, yet their steps never wavering. What happened next caused nothing but fear, chaos, and alarm throughout the entire city of Jericho. As soon as the sandals of the men bearing the Ark touched the river, the water ceased to flow. The water began to separate. The water flowing downstream began to mount up above them leaving the land on which they stood as dry as the bank of the Jordan. It was as if an invisible wall suddenly appeared blocking the water from the bearers of the Ark of the Covenant. The water on the other side of them stilled completely. The valley around the Israelis began to fill with water, but the Ark bearers held their position as the children of Israel began their trek across the Jordan River, now walking across on completely dry land.

Rahab heard the screams of fear rising around her as the people of Jericho began to rush to and fro. Shouts were heard, and alarms within the city sounded as the gates were ordered closed, and the city was placed on lockdown. No one would be allowed to enter the city, and no one would be allowed to leave. They were prisoners in their own land, the gates to the city now being ordered to remain sealed until further notice.

Rahab did not move. She simply stood watching as the entire company of wanderers continued walking across the river, their feet on completely dry ground. She knew with certainty that one of the men on horseback must be Salmon, and she could not help but smile at the thought of him.

Her people were witnessing a miracle of the God she had chosen to serve. Her faith was reaffirmed. Any questions lingering at the back of her mind regarding her decision to follow Jehovah were answered. There was one true God, her God, the God of the Israelites, and He had made Himself known to her and to any willing to attest to the miracle happening before them.

Rahab watched as the final band of travelers crossed onto the shore. At their safe arrival, twelve men returned to the dry riverbed selecting stones from the place the bearers of the Ark remained standing, hoisting the stones onto their shoulders and bringing them into the place the Israelis had begun to make camp. Once they were safely on land, the men bearing the Ark of the Covenant began their own advancement toward land. As soon as the last two bearers were safely on shore, the waters began to flow again with a mighty roar, returning the Jordan to its overflowing stage as before and leaving the valley around them dry once again.

Rahab watched as the twelve stones retrieved from the riverbed were stacked on top of one another, seemingly to form some sort of monument.

"We have witnessed a true miracle," her father spoke in awe. "The time has come. Prepare yourselves," he instructed his younger children, "for a miraculous journey."

Joshua called to the Israelite people standing before him as they settled on this side of the Jordan River. "Today, you have witnessed yet another miracle performed by our awesome God!" he shouted. "Our God has allowed us safe passage over the Jordan River, ensuring us yet again that we are about to reach our Promised Land!" A cheer from his company went up around him. He allowed them to rejoice for a few moments before raising his hands to quiet them.

"The twelve stones which I have pitched in this land will serve as a constant reminder of this victory. When your children shall ask of their fathers in times to come, 'What mean ye these stones,' ye shall let your children know, saying, Israel came over this Jordan on dry land. For the Lord your God dried up the water of Jordan from before you until ye were passed over as the Lord your God did to the Red Sea, which he dried up from before us until we were gone over. That all the people of the earth might know the hand of the Lord, that it is mighty: that ye might fear the Lord your God forever!"

That day, the manna from Heaven ceased to fall, as the children of Israel were able to eat glorious meals of unleavened cakes and parched corn from the fruits of the land of Canaan. Though the wanderers around him celebrated, rejoiced, and praised God for their victory in crossing the Jordan, Joshua retreated to his tent, spending extra time in prayers of thanksgiving and praise, and thanking God for yet another miracle. One more obstacle had been removed which had stood between them and their Promised Land.

Joshua showed no fear, no reserve, and no worry in front of Salmon and the men who would fight alongside him, but deep inside, where only God in Heaven could see, his concern was there. He knew their God would help them prevail and had faith that they would claim the land promised to them, but how? It lay right before them now with nothing between what was promised to them but the walls which were surrounding it. Huge, well-fortified, well-protected, seemingly impenetrable walls.

Joshua prayed himself into exhaustion, relying on the God whom he loved and whom he served to provide him with the answers he needed in due time. Joshua knew that nothing would be revealed to him before God was ready to reveal it, but in that time, when God was ready to miraculously show up, nothing could stop Him. Joshua fell asleep with peace in his heart, not realizing just how quickly those answers and that time would come.

Nazim stoked his campfire and rotated the meat on the spit. He enjoyed this time of solitude. It gave him time to think and reflect on the activities of the past several days. He led his horse to the creek he was camping by, allowing him one more drink for the night. He had made excellent time and should reach the land of Gilead, the land of the Amorites, before nightfall tomorrow. He had been focused on his journey and on the purpose of it, but tonight he could not keep his mind from wandering to Rahab.

Less than a week had passed since their argument. He had said things to her and said things about her that he could never take back. He had expressed anger toward her that neither he nor she had ever experienced. Yet, how could she have betrayed him as she had, and not only him but the people of Jericho as well? It was so unlike her to act in such a manner. She had always been so levelheaded and practical. What had come over her? Or who, he thought with a sigh.

He had tried to do as right by her as he could over the years that he had known her, giving her jewelry and trinkets to make her smile. And he always paid her well. She had known from the beginning that he would never be able to lay claim on her publicly. She knew that he had too much at stake to ruin his reputation in that way. And though he had never meant to hurt her, he had never meant to fall in love with her either.

He laid his head against the trunk of the tree he had settled beside.

When did things become so complicated? he thought to himself. And all this nonsense talk about one God? He scoffed aloud, though something within him stirred at the notion. The feeling troubled him, but he passed it off as his being so tired.

Rahab had never been one prone to flights of fancy. She had never pressed him for more than he was willing to give her. Then, the Israelites had shown up. As if it were not enough that they were such a threat to the city, at least one of them was a direct threat to Nazim himself. He, Salmon, had turned her eye in a direction opposite of what Nazim could give her, and that was what scared him most of all.

Chapter Fifteen

Joshua stood in the midst of the men who would fight with him. The time had come for battle as well as the answers to the questions he had sought.

"Our people are expecting a battle against the inhabitants of Jericho," he spoke to his most trusted group of men, "but the battle will be the Lord's! I have been visited by a Captain of the Host of the Lord, and he has given me clear instructions as to how we will be given the land of Jericho. Carefully follow my instructions and carefully follow my lead," he commanded. "Call the priests together, for today we shall begin our final quest for the battle of our Promised Land!"

Above them, the men of Jericho loomed on the rooftops of their city wall. Since the crossing of the Jordan, the king's centurions had claimed those rooftops and kept watch over the camp of Israelites both day and night. Rahab recognized Jenoah as the soldier who had been watching from her rooftop. She felt like it was no small coincidence he was Nazim's second in command. She longed to ask about him, to know if any word had been sent to this man as to Nazim's whereabouts. Yet she realized to do so would seem impertinent, seeing as how those in town knew her as nothing more than a harlot, and her inquisition of any specific man would call that man out. So, she kept her tongue and her conversation brief as he passed through her inn to her rooftop several times each day and night.

Almost two weeks had passed since Nazim had left to find the answers he sought, and Rahab had prayed for him daily. She prayed for his safety and for his return, but mostly she prayed for him to accept the knowledge of the God she had chosen. She prayed that the people of their city would turn from their wickedness and accept the God of the Israelites. She prayed that they would surrender their city peacefully and be saved from the demise they were about to endure.

All around her, however, she saw the growing wickedness of her people. The miracle they witnessed of their enemies crossing the Jordan had sent them into sheer chaos. With the most notable centurions continuing their focus on the Israelites from the rooftops above, and Nazim's absence being felt by those who so respected him, the people of the city were left to run amuck in the streets bringing nothing but turmoil and grief to the inhabitants. Rahab kept her family close and made sure they stayed very near to her home at all times. If they ventured out, they did so quickly and only to locate and bring back necessary provisions. They must be near in case the attack began.

Everyone was gathered around the table this morning, everyone except her sister. Her mother had searched all the rooms in the inn but had not been able to locate her. Her father had ventured into the street, but she was not to be found. The one place that had not been checked was the rooftop.

Rahab quietly approached and ascended the steps, recognizing her sister's quiet laughter as she approached the roof. She was there, a small cup of water she had brought up for Jenoah resting on the ledge.

"I am sure the soldier appreciates the drink," Rahab interrupted as she reached the rooftop. "Father is looking for you," she revealed as her sister ducked her head and hurried down the steps behind her older sister, her face flaming at being caught.

"She meant no harm, nor did I," Jenoah quickly defended once her sister was out of earshot.

"No harm done," Rahab confirmed as she turned to return to her place inside the inn.

"I have no doubt Nazim cares for you," he spoke quietly, stopping her in her tracks.

"Excuse me?" Rahab questioned stopping on the top step and looking back at him

"He does not realize I have put it all together," he continued, knowing she had heard his first statement clearly.

Rahab dropped her head and turned to go, not willing to get into this conversation with this man who knew Nazim so well.

"It all makes sense to me now," he continued, her curiosity causing her to stop and turn to him once more. "All the times I caught him in the street before, or after, his duty. The anger I saw when Jakabed bragged about speaking with you, and Nazim's quick decision to leave town. I cannot help but feel you have something to do with all of that," he concluded watching the woman in front of him.

Rahab stared at this man before her trying to decide if he was a friend or an enemy.

"I am not saying these things as a threat to you," he clarified, reading the expression on her face, "or to Nazim. I do not know the story between the two of you; I just thought you should know that I feel he really does care."

Rahab turned, walked to the edge of the roof where he stood, and looked over the horizon. The Israeli camp was now right outside the wall. More of the king's soldiers flanked either side of them, not close enough to hear the low tone he was using, but within earshot if voices were to be raised. "The problem with that," she stated simply, "is that he does not care enough."

She turned to go, finished with the conversation she did not wish to begin, but stopped when movement below caught her eye, the same movement capturing Jenoah's attention. A line of men from the Israeli camp had begun to form along the outer wall of the city. Seven men were at the front of the line, each carrying a ram's horn trumpet. Behind them, a golden chest being carried by what appeared to be priests and behind them a host of men who appeared armed and ready for battle.

"Men, prepare yourself!" Jenoah yelled to all around him. Soldiers on both sides of them repeated the shout for any out of Jenoah's direct earshot to hear. Rahab watched as the company of Israeli men began to march, their destination appearing to lie around the city walls. Not a word was being spoken. No threats were being called out, no cries of battle, the ram's horn trumpets did not sound. Nothing was heard except the shuffling of the Israeli men's feet as they continued to march around the city wall.

The men of Jericho were on full alert, watching quietly, and poised for attack, their eyes never leaving the men below them. Rahab spotted Salmon and Garrick in the midst of the line near the front, but they kept their gaze straight ahead, and never wavered in their march. The soldiers of Jericho continued their watch from their places; every soldier's eyes intently following the Israeli men as they continued to place one foot uniformly in front of the other. Completely around the outer wall, they marched, only once, and then turned as they reached their starting point back in the direction of their camp. It seemed they were retreating!

"They are afraid," Rahab heard one of the men of Jericho yell. "They could not find an easy passage through our wall, so they have retreated!" another called. "They fear the soldiers of Jericho!" Great rejoicing was heard inside the city walls, but Rahab noticed that Jenoah did not join in the celebration.

"I must speak with the king," he began, as he left the roof in haste. Rahab watched as he moved quickly toward the palace, then turned her attention again to the Israeli camp. Standing alone and looking directly at her from his place below was Salmon. Everyone else had left the roof, rejoicing in the retreat of their enemy, so no one but Rahab saw as he lifted both of his hands to his lips then held them in her direction. She recognized it for the signal that it was. In some way, the battle had begun.

Nazim slammed the mug on the table in front of him, clearly frustrated at reaching another dead end. Every avenue he had taken, every shred of information he had been given had ended up useless. It seemed a God who was invincible led this wayward band of Israeli travelers. Every obstacle they had encountered in their quest for their Promised Land had been rendered useless. He could find nothing that would point him to any sort of weakness that would assure Jericho a victory over them. Nazim was about to agree with Rahab; perhaps they should surrender their home peacefully. He rolled his eyes at his utterly absurd, foolish notion.

He still could not rid her from his mind where she haunted him day and night, and that frustrated him all the more. He had even gone so far as to spend an evening with someone else in an attempt to replace her, but the harlot fell very short in comparison to Rahab. Though his physical desires had been temporarily quenched, he had left the woman's bed feeling void. He realized the mental attachment he had made to Rahab had far surpassed the physical attachment, but the betrayal she had engaged in and the words he had spoken to her could never be forgiven. Still, he knew he would have to try.

He would stay in this foreign land for one day more before returning to Jericho. If nothing hindered his travel, he would be back home within six days. Once he arrived before he sought out the king, and before he sought out Jenoah for a briefing, he would seek out Rahab and attempt to make things right with her. If she were willing to forgive him for his harsh words and explosive anger and give up her foolish notion of siding with the Israelites and serving their God, he would forgive her for her betrayal. Things could go back to the way they were between them. Then, somehow, he would lead the men of Jericho in a victorious battle, and they would defeat the Israelites.

Any of his men were welcome to kill any and as many of the Israeli soldiers as they wanted. Except for one, the man called Salmon. That man, Nazim had decided, would be his own personal conquest.

Jenoah stood before the king where he sat on his throne relishing in what he considered a victory, through no work of his own.

"Relax, Jenoah," the King commanded, with a wave of his hand. "Revel in the victory! The Israelites have retreated!" he rejoiced.

"To their camp, your Highness," Jenoah explained again, his fingers pinching the bridge of his nose. "There is no indication of the Israelites going anywhere. I feel this march was some sort of a signal, a warning perhaps, to the war we face."

"Give them time to lick their wounds," the king argued. "They are taking time to grieve over their loss, realizing a battle with the mighty men of Jericho is just too much," he smirked, "even for their God. No doubt they will be gone by morning." He held his arms wide. "Look at this place, Jenoah," he bragged. "We are the most fortified city in the nation. They marched themselves around our wall and realized it was a useless feat. Now," he began as he stood from his place and walked toward the soldier in front of him, "you are bringing me down, and I do not appreciate the negativity. Go. Relax and rejoice. It is a command," he spoke by way of dismissing him.

Jenoah bowed and turned from the foolish man before him. He could argue with the king all day, but he would never make him see. Something was very wrong; he just could not figure out exactly what it was.

As he left the palace, one question plagued him more than all others. "Where are you, Nazim?" he thought aloud. He wanted nothing more at this moment than to seek council from his most trusted ally.

Chapter Sixteen

The next morning Jenoah returned to his place on the rooftop, still unable to shake the feeling that there was more going on with the Israelites than his fellow comrades cared to see. He knew they would not give up so easily. Too much fear had been struck in the heart of Jericho for these men to give up the land that they claimed had been promised to them so quickly. And what of their God? Had he perhaps abandoned them, leaving them to fight the battle alone? Perhaps He had tired of them, and His miracles had ceased, and that was the reason for their retreat. Jenoah hoped the King was right and that he would gain the rooftop this morning only to see that the Israelites camp had been abandoned and that they had moved on to some other land. Unfortunately, as he had predicted, that was not the case.

As he watched, the line of Israeli men began to form once again. Just as before, seven men bearing ram's horn trumpets were at the front of the line, followed by the priests bearing the golden chest, and following them, their men of battle. Rahab joined him on the roof as the line formed, and as they watched, again the march began. Others from the city took notice, and a deathly quiet fell again upon the city, nothing being heard but the shuffling of the Israelites feet as they marched around the outer wall.

The soldiers of Jericho stood ready once more to fight, but after the company had marched around the wall only once, they again turned, returning to their camp. No shouts, no blare of the trumpets, no threats of battle, just their simple march, one time around the wall.

Jenoah sighed and turned to leave, shaking his head in confusion. He had not spoken to Rahab, where she stood beside him taking in the scene as well.

"Have you word from him?" she asked, feeling brave enough to ask since he had called her out the day before.

"I have not," he spoke honestly, knowing exactly the "him" she was speaking of, "though I surely wish I had," he finished as he exited the roof.

Rahab watched him leave and turned again to look over the horizon. As the day before, Salmon stood alone looking in her direction, and as the day before he lifted his hand to his mouth before he held it high for her to see. Yet today there was something slightly different. It was a fleeting notion, nothing specific she could put her finger on.

She thought for a moment as she replayed the gesture in her mind and then dismissed her curiosity. Perhaps it was nothing more than his promise to her that she had not been forgotten.

Nazim walked into the establishment he had been staying at for the past few weeks. He had planned to leave town the day before, but one last bit of information had been discovered, and he had stayed behind to check it out. Yet again, he was disappointed, as it only served in detaining him for nothing.

The day had been long, and he wanted nothing but a meal, a bath, and a bed. The woman he had spent the one night with before approached him as he ate, but he simply held his hand up and shook his head no. She was not prone to begging and simply moved on to the next lonely looking man she saw.

Nazim was finishing his meal when one of his so-called informants approached him.

"Still here?" he asked, welcoming himself to Nazim's table.

Nazim never answered or even acknowledged the man. He took another drink from his mug and pushed his chair back to leave, throwing some coins on the table to pay for his fare as he did so. This man had been no help to him before, and Nazim did not assume he would begin to now. He wiped his mouth as he gave the man a menacing look and stood to go to his room.

"You might want to hurry," the man spoke carelessly around a bite of bread, "we have heard those Israelites you are seeking information about are on the move."

Nazim turned to look over his shoulder at the husky man as he continued to sit, stuffing another spoonful of meat into his mouth.

"Do not waste my time with useless information again," Nazim demanded, "but if you have something worth saying, then say it," he spoke plainly. The man scoffed, and Nazim felt his patience weighing heavily where this imbecile was concerned.

"My sources tell me the city of Jericho is under lockdown," he spoke without looking at Nazim. "No one going in, and no one coming out."

"Since when?" Nazim asked, his curiosity piqued. That made no sense.

"Since the Israelites crossed over the Jordan River," he said as though it were a natural occurrence, pausing to take another bite of bread. "On dry land," he finally finished, cutting his eyes to where Nazim stood above him.

Nazim moved so quickly the chair he was standing near toppled over. Grabbing the man by the neck of his tunic, he lifted him partly from his chair.

"Are you lying to me?" he asked through clenched teeth as the man he held labored to breathe. Other visitors to the inn moved away from the tables surrounding them, giving Nazim all the room he needed.

"I am not," he stuttered. "Traveling merchants have been sent away from the city, not being allowed entry. My source told me the people of Jericho witnessed the miracle." His face was turning red, and his speech was impaired. Nazim released him, causing his chair to topple over and the man to spill into the floor.

"When did this take place," he asked his hands clenched into tight fists by his side. He would not even have to dirty his sword on this coward were the need to arise.

The man rubbed his neck from his place on the floor but did not move to get up.

"He said it happened a couple of days ago. He just returned to town today!" he spoke quickly as Nazim moved toward him thinking he had been withholding information. "He made a stop to sell his wares on his way back!" he stammered in defense.

Nazim stared at the lump of nothing cowering in the floor in front of him. The way he claimed to have gotten his information made sense enough, and Nazim believed the man was telling him the truth this time.

"My horse," Nazim called to the innkeeper as he stepped over the man now attempting to rise from the floor. Turning back, he dropped some coins in front of him as he struggled to rise.

"For the information," he clarified without a smile.

Within minutes, Nazim was on the back of his horse racing back to Jericho. It would take him four days in the best of circumstances to get back to the city. He did not have a moment to lose.

Every day the march was the same. The men of the Israelite camp would form a line with the ram's horn trumpet bearers at the head, followed by the men bearing the golden box, and then the men of battle. One march, around the city walls, and then the company would retreat to their camp. Rahab would stand on the rooftop and wait for the signal she expected from Salmon each day. It was on the third day of the single march that she realized that he was sending her a message.

Each day, after the march was completed and they had retreated to their camp, Salmon would touch his hand to his mouth, and then hold it in the direction where Rahab stood watching. Anyone who witnessed the gesture, other than Rahab, might assume the man was praising God for another successful march, but Rahab realized the signal was meant for her.

On the day of the first march, Salmon had used both of his hands, holding up six of his fingers. She had paid no attention then. On the second day, one hand, all five fingers held high. It still did not click with her until the third day. On the third day of their single march, she realized that Salmon had held up one less finger. It was a countdown. Each day, Rahab knew that she and her family were one day closer to their day of redemption, but her city was one day closer to their demise. She kept her realization to herself, not even telling her family. She felt to do so would break the promise she had made to Salmon when she had hidden him on this very rooftop; the promise that she would not give away the Israeli's plan.

Their city was in complete turmoil, this game the Israelite's were playing with them was wearing on the minds and the hearts of not only the soldiers but the inhabitants of Jericho as well. Rahab had no doubt that if Nazim had been present, he would have already orchestrated an attack against the Israelis. Patience had never been his strong point, and he was never prone to waiting to see what would happen.

Finally, the daily march took place for the sixth time. The formation of the men was the same. Not a sound was made other than their marching. As was normal, Salmon stood outside the camp, but today, he was also smiling as he did so. He raised his hand to his lips then held it out toward Rahab, slowly lowering the one finger he held high, just as she had expected. Tomorrow was the day of battle.

Chapter Seventeen

Nazim woke with a start, jolting upright with such force that his horse jumped where he was tied near him. The dream was over, but the incredible sense of dread was very real and very present. He had not wanted to stop, but his horse could not take another step. He knew he had ridden him too hard for too long. He had only planned to break for an hour, to give his steed water and a short rest, but while doing so, he himself had fallen into a deep, yet fitful sleep.

He shook his head, trying to dispel the image the dream had left in his mind. Rahab was screaming, calling for him from her window, flames surrounding her. As he watched, the back of a man bearing the torch which had been used in starting the fire continued walked away from her and away from Jericho. That man himself. The dream was so real in his mind that he could feel the smoke he had watched surrounding her burning into his lungs.

He pulled the leather strap from his hair and walked to the river he had stopped by. He leaned over, took a drink, and then splashed the cool water onto his face, in an attempt to force his mind to dispel the images that continued to linger there. Though his head began to clear, the dreadful feeling continued to burn his chest. Something was very, very wrong.

Mounting his horse again, he urged him forward at a pace much faster than he intended to but felt he had no choice. He had to get back to Jericho and back to Rahab. Nazim feared he had been still for too long.

Rahab rose before the sun the next day. She was not sure what all was about to transpire, but she knew from the feeling in her gut and from the signals Salmon had given her the past six days that whatever it was, it would happen today.

She crossed the room to the window where the scarlet cord still hung, making sure it was tight and completely visible to the outside world. Her instructions from Salmon had been clear, and the cord had not been moved since the night he and Garrick had used it to climb to safety. Satisfied she had done as she had been told, she pulled her shawl tight about her body and crept quietly to the rooftop so as not to wake her family. They would need their rest.

Standing here looking over the horizon, she took in the beautiful sight before her. The God she now served had created this, she thought as the sun began to rise, turning the sky into hues of blue, pink and purple.

She looked toward the outskirts of town and wondered of Nazim. He had not yet returned, and a part of her was glad of that fact. For one, she was not sure she was ready to face him again after their argument, really what else was there to say? But two, and probably most truthful of her emotions, if he was not here, she knew he could not die here.

Salmon had told her that everyone within the city walls, save herself and those within her home, would be destroyed. She knew without a doubt, for more reasons than one, that Nazim would not have been among those in the safety of her sanctuary. As she turned her attention back to the Israeli camp, she saw the first stirrings of the morning. Women had begun to venture from their tents, awakening their fires in order to prepare morning meals.

Though she realized that whatever happened today would be God's will, she knew that the day would not be an easy one. She prayed her heart was ready for whatever was to come.

Jenoah approached quietly taking his place on the rooftop. She glanced at him for a moment and then turned her attention back to the Israelites. "My heart aches this morning for reasons I cannot identify," he admitted to her. She stood in silence, toying with the pendant around her neck, seeing no reason for words. The feeling of dread was heavy on them all.

As the sun broke over the horizon, the Israeli's formed their line to march. It was the seventh time they had watched this scene unfold. Like every day for the past six days, the soldiers of Jericho lined the rooftops, poised for battle and watching carefully. Rahab's family appeared. It seemed everyone had a sense that something different would take place today.

As the Israelites approached the wall for the seventh time, Rahab sought out Salmon as she had every day, watching him take his place in the formation and watching as the company begin their familiar march once again. The quiet ensued as always, and no matter how long she lived Rahab knew she would never forget the sound of the shuffling soldiers' feet as the Israelis marched around their city.

Rahab watched as the king's soldiers turned to leave as the familiar march neared completion.

"Hold your positions," Jenoah shouted, causing each of the retreating men to pause and turn back. The priests who bore the ram's horn trumpets had not turned to lead the host of men back to their camp today but instead continued a second march around the wall.

All of Jericho watched with bated breath as the company of men marched twice, then three times around the wall. Four times. Five, six, and seven treks around the wall they marched; all the while the only sound being made was the shuffling of Israeli feet.

"What are they doing?" Rahab heard murmured time and again by those who had gathered around them. The men of Jericho were growing impatient when finally, after their seventh completed march around the outer wall, the Israelites stopped in their tracks turning and facing the great wall looming before them.

All of Jericho held their breath, except for Rahab. She knew whatever was about to happen was about to happen fast. Something overtook her, and she knew she had to follow Salmon's instructions and get her family inside the safety of her house.

"Quickly!" she spoke aloud to her parents, sister, and brothers, causing everyone around her to jump as she broke the silence. "Get into the house, now!" She looked to Jenoah, offering him safety without saying a word. He returned her gaze, the confusion evident on his face, and she gave him only a second before she turned following her family as they raced down the steps and into the safety of the inn.

Rahab went straight to the window where the scarlet cord hung brightly, dancing in the morning sun that was now high above them. Each of the Israelite men held their position, staring at the wall. Rahab kept her place in the window, observing in fear as the scene began to unfold. Later, she wished she had hidden in an inner room with the rest of her family instead of witnessing all she was about to.

Slowly, the priests bearing the ram's horn trumpets lifted them to their lips and blew. Another sound Rahab knew she would never forget. Long blasts filled the air and along with them the shouts of the men of Israel.

"Shout!" Joshua called to his people, from his place on horseback among them. "For the Lord hath given you the city. And the city shall be accursed, even it, and all that are therein, to the Lord: only Rahab the harlot shall live, she and all that are with her in the house because she hid the messengers that we sent.

"And ye, in any wise keep yourselves from the accursed thing, lest ye make yourselves accursed, when ye take of the accursed thing, and make the camp of Israel a curse, and trouble it. But all the silver, and gold, and vessels of brass and iron, are consecrated unto the Lord: they shall come unto the treasury of the Lord."

Suddenly, as the trumpets continued to blare, and the men continued their shout, the ground beneath all of Jericho began to shake. Gently at first, and then more viciously, trembling violently until nothing could stand upon it. Rahab held to the windowsill as her inn trembled, noticing the walls around them begin to crumble. Yet, her section of the wall stood strong.

She heard the people of Jericho scream as they toppled from the rooftops of their city to their death below and the earth-shattering sound of the outer walls as they crashed around them. Rahab ran to her window facing the street and observed as the walls all around the city continue to give way section by section, collapsing onto the people who ran through the streets below them seeking shelter they would not find. Dust and debris filled the air as the heavy stones continued to crash to the ground. Finally, nothing was left standing or untouched; nothing, save Rahab's wall.

At the demise of the outer wall, the ground stilled its quaking, the barrier between the city and the Israelite army now completely obliterated. The Israeli's continued their battle cry, as they begin an easy climb over the piles of stone and mud scaling the debris easily and slaughtering anyone in their path.

Many of the people of Jericho who had felt so secure inside their impenetrable walls now lay crumpled and dead beneath them. The idolatrous gods they had spent their lives worshipping and serving now lay helpless and crushed beneath the walls of the tabernacle. Rahab felt her heart break as she saw her city being overtaken. She had prayed for a better way, but it was not to be. She longed to turn away from all she was seeing, but she could not force her eyes from the vision outside her windows.

Jenoah had remained safe on her rooftop and now flew down the stairs, his heart taken over by implacable anger upon hearing Joshua call out that Rahab would be spared for her aid in saving the spies.

"YOU!" he shouted, upon finding her by the window. She turned in the direction of his voice. "You protected the spies!" he seethed in anger. "Now, there is no one to protect you! Nazim will forgive me when he hears of your treachery," he pledged as he rushed forward, drawing his sword. Rahab held fast to the windowsill as he came, her parents and siblings screaming in terror as he advanced toward her. Then, as suddenly as he had arrived, he stopped and fell face-first onto the floor in front of her. Behind him stood Salmon. Jenoah lay motionless with Salmon's hatchet lodged firmly in his back.

"Let's go," Salmon instructed, reaching his hand out to her.

"Follow me!" Garrick yelled right behind him, motioning for her family. Her siblings and parents wasted no time in following Garrick as he beckoned, but Rahab stood in her place as sobs overtook her body. It was too much. She was frozen where she stood, save her sobbing, one hand covering her face, the other clutching the pendent ever present on her chest; the pendent Nazim had given her not so many months ago. It was the last connection she had to him, the last connection she had to the city, her city, which now lay in ruins around her.

Salmon recognized her reserve, and unlike Nazim would have, he approached her calmly amid the chaos. The turmoil around them seemed to cease as he spoke as if they were the only two people left in the world.

"The time is now, Rahab," he said softly. "I promised you safety, and safety is what I have come to offer you."

She continued clutching the pendant at her neck. "I cannot," she cried, "I am no better than the rest of my people. I do not deserve your God or your protection," she continued to sob. "I am nothing more than a harlot. I cannot go with you, Salmon," she lowered her head, her tears coming in a torrent.

"You can," he promised. "I am right here to help you." He moved to her gently framing her face with his hands. "Look at me," he demanded, lifting her chin, forcing her to lift her eyes to his. He knew she was in shock. Softly he continued to caress her face as he spoke.

"You were a harlot, but you have been forgiven of your sins. There is nothing you can ever do that can separate you from the love of God," he promised her. "You cannot outrun Him, you cannot hide from Him, you cannot ignore that He is here, and I know that you really do not want to. Come with me. Leave this world and these memories behind you."

Rahab looked into his face and nodded her head. He wiped the tears continuing to stream along her cheeks and let her go, though he did not turn from her; he simply began to back away, never taking his eyes from her hers, as she stood with her back to the windowsill still clutching and caressing the pendant at her neck.

"Come with me," he urged gently, holding his hand out to her once again.

Rahab closed her eyes and rubbed the pendant as everything that had happened over the past few months came flooding back to her mind. She thought of the void feeling she had experienced for years that had suddenly been filled when she had accepted the God of the Israelites. She thought of the life she had with Nazim, an incomplete life that had been going nowhere and was filled with more lonely nights than shared moments. She thought of Salmon rescuing her outside the city walls, not only from the man who sought to harm her but also as he told her for the first time of his God. She thought of the conversations they had shared as she prepared to hide him on her roof. She thought of the words Nazim had said to her when she had tried so desperately to share her God with him, and she thought of the signals Salmon had constantly sent to her over the past week as he reassured her not only that he would be coming for her, but that their God would be protecting her as well.

She realized the peace and freedom she had so often longed for had come from none other than God above. It did not rest with Salmon, though she knew God had sent him to her, and it certainly did not rest with Nazim. God had never forsaken her, even before she realized her need for Him, and she would not forsake Him. Not now, not ever.

She opened her eyes to see Salmon, continuing to stand patiently before her, his hand still extended. Rahab knew that she had to let the chains go, the chains that had bound her for so long. The chains of guilt from her past, the chains that held her to Nazim, and most importantly, the chains that were holding her here. Suddenly, she gave the chain about her neck a fierce tug, and the clasp broke free. Holding it her hands, she rubbed the pendant once more, before looking into the eyes of the man who waited to take her to safety. She knew what she had to do. Forcefully, she laid the chain and pendant on the table by the window that had remained upright and untouched, and without looking back, reached out, taking Salmon's hand. And they ran.

When they reached the street, Salmon quickly mounted his horse, pulling Rahab up in front of him in one quick motion, her legs draping over one side of the stallion. Screams and battle-cries reached her ears as the men of Israel continued to claim the city that was rightfully theirs, and she lowered her eyes from the scene continuing to take place around them.

"Do not look back," Salmon advised as he placed his arms on either side of her taking the reins and holding her firmly. She turned, circling his waist with her arms and burying her face into his chest as he urged the horse into motion, quickly maneuvering the stallion through the chaotic streets and away from the ruins of the city.

Once they were in the safety of the Israelite camp, and she was reunited with her family, Salmon left them in the care of the Israeli women and returned to the battlefield. There he aided the men in retrieving the gold, silver, brass, and iron for the Lord's treasury.

When everything had been retrieved, fire was set to the remnants of Jericho except the wall where Rahab's home had been. That wall would remain intact, a clear sign to anyone who approached, that a promise had been kept by the Israelites and by the God they served.

Rahab sat inside the Israeli camp with her back to the city, refusing to look behind her. Instead, she chose to only look forward, facing her future.

Two days later, Nazim stood alone in the only portion of the wall that did not lie in heaps of stone and ash around him. The city he had so adamantly attempted to protect lay in ruins. He had been miles away when the smoke had become visible, as he had raced toward the city. His heart failed to beat as he realized his efforts had been in vain. He was too late.

He could not comprehend how it had happened as he led his horse through the abandoned streets. Suddenly, he noticed one portion of the wall still standing. Approaching that section, he realized it had been the section of the wall where Rahab had resided. As he ran up the steps, his feet barely made contact as he took them two by two. He had prayed as he went, though to whom he was uncertain, that he would find her hiding inside, but alas, his prayer was in vain.

A sound behind him caused his heart to skip a beat, and he quickly realized it was only pieces of the scarlet cord flapping in the breeze from where it hung. He touched the remnants of the cord as if it were a treasure and could not help but notice that the majority of it had been cut away. He looked around the room for the larger piece of it, but it was not to be found. Instead, another treasure caught his eye.

He could not stop the tears of frustration that filled his eyes when the pendant caught his eye where it lay on a table by the window near where the cord had hung. Gently he picked it up, rubbing the smooth stone between his fingers as he remembered the day that he had given it to her. A gift she had at first rejected, and then cherished, though here it lay rejected once again. This pendant did give him assurance of one thing, however, he realized as he fingered the broken clasp. He was certain that Rahab was alive.

He tucked the pendant into the pocket of his vest and allowed himself one more glance around the room. This room where he had spent so much of his time, the room she had once brought such life to, the same room where he had enjoyed so much laughter and pleasure. A thought occurred to him as he thought back, and his thoughts moved from himself to Rahab. He could not help but wonder how much pleasure she had actually experienced here. This room, no doubt, had held more disappointment and heartache for her than joy and laughter. Sadness and grief, no doubt, filled her memories, memories of the nights he had left her, the mornings she had awakened alone, the men she had tolerated, and the death of the one woman she had considered a friend. He was certain the memories here were not at all pleasant for Rahab as they had been for him.

Mounting his horse and turning from the town, he made a vow to whatever God was around to hear it. He would find her. He would find Rahab, he would find the Israelite who took her from him, and he would find the God who had orchestrated it all, and there was nothing under the heavens that would stop him

Chapter Eighteen

Two weeks had passed since Rahab and her family had joined the Israeli camp. Most of the time, she had slept, the stress and worries of the past few weeks catching up with her. This morning she felt more like herself than she had in months, and she longed to stretch her legs and move about the camp.

Surprisingly, she and her family had been taken in and accepted graciously by the Israelites. Her mother had befriended several of the older ladies and was eager to learn all they would teach her of their ways of completing everyday tasks. Her father could often be found in deep spiritual discussions with men who knew much about the God they served, as they informed him of their beliefs and practices in serving and worshipping the one true God of the universe. Her brothers had found friendships with some of the younger men in the group; playing games they had created throughout their time in the wilderness and assisting them with everyday chores, while her sister had formed another sort of attachment, preferring to spend her time with Garrick, who clearly enjoyed the attention he was receiving from her.

Rahab wandered to the banks of the river and sat listening to the water as it passed melodically over the rocks beneath. The sound soothed her, and she watched as the trees swayed in the gentle breeze. Her hand went habitually to her chest, realizing at once that the pendant was gone. She thought of it often, and though in truth it brought a twinge of sadness, it reminded her that the "chains" of her past had been broken as well. She was free. She did not attempt to stop the smile the spread across her face at the gentle reminder. Instead, she toyed with the braid she wore across her shoulder.

She heard someone approach behind her, but felt completely safe inside the Israeli camp and allowed whoever it was to come closer before she turned. It was not unusual for Salmon to check on her several times a day. She had looked forward to the short conversations they had shared as he checked on her wellbeing. She recognized the space he was giving her to rest and to heal. Her smile widened when she saw it was he who now stood beside her.

"I am glad to see you are out and about," he spoke quietly kneeling beside her. "I hope I am not disturbing you."

"Not at all, please sit," she offered. "I have no bread to offer you today," she laughed as she thought of the last time they sat casually together in an open space.

"None needed," he laughed in return, settling close beside her.

They sat in companionable silence for several moments, each enjoying the beauty in nature surrounding them. It was Salmon who spoke first.

"Are you well, Rahab?" he questioned, and she could detect the sincere concern in his voice.

"I am quite well," she answered honestly. "For a few days, I was not so sure, Things have changed so quickly," she admitted. "But seeing my family so accepted by a people who were at one time considered our enemies and being surrounded by those same caring and loving people who seek nothing but peace and favor from the God you have taught us of, has brought a peace and contentment to my heart that I cannot explain," she finished. She had not looked at Salmon as she spoke, instead, keeping her gaze on the river before them. He had done the same, enjoying the fact that she was near him and seemed at peace.

"I have not thanked you," she spoke again, turning to look at him.

"Thanked me?" he questioned with a grin, returning her gaze.

"You saved me," she began, "in so many ways." She turned her attention back to the river as she continued to speak. "From the man outside the city gates, from Jenoah on the day of the attack, but most importantly when you told me of your God," she continued. "As I stood in the windowsill the day you came for me, my city literally crashing around us, I thought back over the course of my life. I have done so many things, Salmon, so many things I could never be proud of, and though I had previously accepted your God the thoughts of those things began to crowd in around me, reminding me of the life I had lived. I realized that I was in no way worthy of the salvation you had told me of. I was no better than the rest of my people, the people who perished right outside my window. The people who were dying without the God whom I had accepted." She turned to him again as she continued. "Thank you, for your patient way of convincing me, of reminding me, of the goodness and graciousness of our God," she finished as tears glistened in her eyes. "Thank you for sharing that saving knowledge with me."

Salmon turned to fully face her. "May I?" he asked, reaching for her hand. As he took her hand, he held it, along with his own, upright between them. Placing his fingers gently against hers, he began.

"None of us are worthy of the love and mercy God has shown to us, Rahab," he spoke slowly. "It is only by the goodness and mercy of God that any of us are here and have the possibility of a life lived with Him. We will fail Him every day, but He is just and quick to forgive. The secret," he continued as he slowly interlocked his fingers with hers, "is to fully place your hand in the hand of our all-knowing, ever-present God. Once you fully surrender your life and your will to Him, there is no power of hell that can pluck you from His hand. Nor mine," he concluded softly.

Only then did Rahab realize how gently he caressed her hand as he spoke and how close his face was to hers. Realizing the same, he looked away, breaking the trance.

"I have something for you," he spoke as he turned, pulling a fold of fabric from where it had been safely tucked in his belt. No longer wound into the cord she had constructed to lead he and Garrick to safety, he handed her a large section of the scarlet material she had so loved.

Rahab caught her breath, her hands going to her mouth. She could not stop the tears that threatened to spill from her eyes.

"I wanted to give it to you sooner," he explained, "but I wanted it to be smooth before I did. Your mother assisted me in unwinding it and attempting to get it back to a condition you could possibly use."

"When? How?" she asked, now holding the fabric in her hands and not being able to get the words out.

Salmon chuckled; pleased he had rendered her speechless.

"When I returned to the city to aid the men in retrieving the metals for the Lord's treasury," he answered, knowing her question without her finishing it. "I could not bear to leave it behind, knowing how much it had meant to you. I will be honest, Rahab," he spoke truthfully. "I left the pendant. I felt the significance of the chain you broke was better left in Jericho."

Rahab held the precious material carefully, amazed at the thoughtfulness of this man before her. There were so many things she could say, but no words could capture the gratitude she felt toward this man at this moment. Laying the material carefully in her lap, she now reached for his hand, which he gladly gave. Replaying the events earlier, she placed their hands as they were before, interlocking her fingers with his.

"Thank you," she spoke simply. It was enough. Salmon looked from her eyes to her mouth. When she did not back away, he leaned forward briefly brushing her lips with his own. His kiss was soft and gentle.

"I am not, nor will I ever be Nazim," he spoke as he pulled away after the very brief kiss.

"If Nazim was who I wanted, I would not have remained in your camp," she answered honestly. "I do not fear being alone; I would have gone in search of him. And though I pray he finds God someday, I have realized that Nazim and I did not have a future together. Only a past," she paused. "I was just not sure you could ever accept me as I was," she finished.

Salmon looked deep into her eyes. "I accept you as you are," he emphasized. "I find myself very taken with you, Rahab," he warned.

"I fear I may be falling quickly," he smiled truthfully.

"As am I," she laughed as he leaned in for another brief kiss.

They returned to the camp not long after, hand in hand, the beautiful fabric draped across Rahab's shoulder.

"That color will look beautiful on you," her mother confirmed thankful at seeing her daughter so content. "Salmon was adamant that we restore it to a condition in which it could be used."

"I have loved this material from the moment I dyed it," she smiled as she held it tenderly. "I had always planned to hold onto it for a special occasion, and I thought it had served its purpose," she admitted.

"I feel there will be another occasion very soon worthy of its wear," her mother chided. "You should get busy," she teased her daughter.

Rahab went to work almost immediately, and less than a month later she wore the beautiful scarlet creation on her wedding day. It was a glorious affair, all of the Israeli's joining in celebration as Salmon and Rahab joined their lives together in the presence of their friends, their families and most importantly, their God.

Rahab knew she would never forget the past that would always plague her. She would never forget Nazim and the relationship they had shared, and she prayed that he would find peace and happiness as she had found in the God she had come to serve.

Her future was clear with a man beside her who held no shame in his love of her. He did not try to possess her, but he cherished her. He did not command her, but he instructed her. He did not lead her by force, but he led her with tenderness, and she would never forget the day he led her to the God who held all wisdom and righteousness. The God she now served, who had taken her sins, though they were as scarlet, and washed them, whiter than snow.

One Year Later

Nazim crept quietly through the wooded area. He had left his horse behind so as to remain completely hidden. He heard her laughter before he saw her. He had been close for months, but now he knew he had finally found her. He had not forgotten her; he would never forget her.

Stealthily he poked his head from behind the massive trunk he was lurking behind. Rahab stood by the water's edge, more beautiful than he remembered, though different somehow. He simply stared at her for a moment, reveling in her beauty. Her hair was wound into a knot at the back of her head. Nazim had always remembered it down, either freely or in a braid. Never had he seen her wear it tied on the back of her neck as it was now. Still, she was breathtaking.

She seemed to be in pleasant conversation with someone, but with whom he could not see and could not make out the words. He longed to be closer. He moved to gain a better vantage point, and as he shuffled, he noticed her head come up as if she felt someone watching her. A voice to her right distracted her, and he saw the smile he missed so desperately brighten her face. *It must be the Israelite*, he thought as he reached to pull an arrow from the quiver on his back. He had waited more than a year for this moment. He would wait until the man was in plain view to assure a clean shot. He had come to take back what was his, that which had been taken from him over a year ago.

"Someone is about to want his mother," the Israelite cheerfully announced as he came into clear view. Nazim stopped.

"What is it, my boy?" Rahab questioned, the smile still present on her face. "Come to mama," she exclaimed laughter filling her voice. "Another of God's precious miracles." At seeing his mother, the infant in the Israelite's arms began to fuss.

"I believe he is hungry," Salmon announced handing the baby to his mother.

"My poor, poor little Boaz," Rahab cooed taking the infant from his father. "You ate less than an hour ago," she chided as she gently began to sway with him, rocking and calming him. The child quieted as she did so.

"We should return so you can feed him," Salmon spoke as he gently kissed her. Nazim noticed the Israelite looking around them as

Rahab continued her gaze on the baby in her arms.

"It is so pleasant here," she pleaded, too caught up in her son to notice her companion's uneasy posture. "Can we not stay a few moments more?" Salmon relinquished, kissing the tip of her nose and grinning as he did so.

"As long as you're comfortable feeding him here," he agreed.

"I do not believe he is hungry," she admitted. "I believe he is only tired." Rahab continued to sway with her son, singing softly in his ear as she did so, the infant nestling in her arms as she rocked him to sleep.

"I will be right back," Salmon excused himself, dropping a kiss on her cheek. He did not wish to alarm his wife, but he knew they were being watched.

Nazim lowered his bow and his gaze. Rahab had a son. Even he could not leave a child so young without a father. The Israelite had left her side, but Nazim could not bring himself to move from the shadows. How would she react at seeing him again? Would she run to him? Would she run from him?

He did not get a chance to find out. Looking in her direction once again, someone behind her caught his eye. Staring straight at him was the Israelite, his arms crossed, his look menacing. He would protect his wife and his child at any cost. Nazim saw the warning there. He knew this man would not make a scene unless he had to. He also recognized that the fight would be an even one. This man was equal to his own size, and the look on his face proved he was not afraid.

For the first time in his life, Nazim put Rahab's needs and desires before his own. He heeded the warning from Salmon, dropped his head, and turned to walk quietly away.

He had sought out Rahab, found her, and he realized he had lost her. He had sought out the Israelite, found him, and left him alone without a fight. Nazim recognized the only thing he had left to search for was the one being that eluded him the most. He would search for Him, and he would find Him if it took the rest of his life. He would begin his journey in earnest, and he would not rest until he found the God who started it all.

Closing Thoughts

"We Have Heard" is a historical fiction account of the life of Rahab but is based upon actual events. This book has been by far, the most fun of all the books I have written to this point. I have fallen completely in love with the characters of this book, the real ones and the fictional ones, and I am going to miss spending time with them each day.

So little was said about Rahab in the Bible, and I had such liberty to expand her character. I enjoyed getting to know her and cannot wait to talk with her in Heaven someday. She is the perfect example of how God can take a life of sin and turn it into a life for Him. God redeemed Rahab and used her in the genealogy of Christ. There is no honor greater than that.

Salmon had to be one of the most loving and forgiving men ever created. He looked beyond Rahab's past to the woman of God she would become and loved her completely and fully. Not many men could do that.

And that brings me to Nazim, my fictional character, whom I became completely devoted to saving. I could not let him die in Jericho. I agonized over a way to get him out of the city while staying true to the story, which is laid out so plainly in the Bible. He was the most exciting character I have ever created, and I truly hope to expand his character by using his own story in a stand-alone book someday. Nazim, the "bad boy" of my mind, who needs nothing more

211

to than to find the God he now searches for and come to know Jesus. Which brings me to my point.

It doesn't matter what evil you have done. It doesn't matter the sin you have entertained or been a part of. God will not reject you. You can be saved.

On the other hand, you can be as good as you want to be and you can live a life as pure as you want to, but you cannot get to Heaven without the saving knowledge of Jesus Christ.

You cannot "turn over a new leaf" and expect to be pure enough. You cannot do enough good deeds and expect to be good enough.

The deed was done, on a cross, over 2,000 years ago when Jesus gave His life to save wretched sinners. Sinners like Rahab, Salmon, and Nazim. Sinners like me and sinners like you.

Fortunately, we live a world where "We Have Heard" the gospel message time and again. If you are looking for a way to break the chains that bind you, if you are searching for peace in a world filled with chaos, then look no further than Jesus Christ. He will fill you with a peace that passes all understanding and lead you straight to the gates of Heaven.

And if by chance you have not heard of the saving knowledge of Jesus Christ or would like to know more, tune in to our church services on Facebook live each Sunday at 11:00am and 6:00pm and on Wednesday evenings at 7:00 pm. Cornerstone Baptist Church of Mooresboro, NC. Let us know you're watching!

Other Books in this Series

When Angels Speak

The Prudent Queen